MONSTER ACADEMY FOR THE MAGICAL: HIDDEN MAGIC

(MONSTER ACADEMY FOR THE MAGICAL, #2)

JESSICA SORENSEN

HAVEN

I AM THE MOST CURSED GIRL IN THE WORLD.

Or, well, monster …

Monster.

I am a monster.

As I sit here in this cage, the reality of the situation starts to really hit me.

I had always wondered if I was a monster, but it was more metaphorical. I didn't actually believe I was a real monster. I didn't think real monsters existed.

But now there's no denying it.

Monsters exist.

And I am one.

I'm not sure how long I remain stuck in the cage by myself, replaying all the signs that should've helped me figured it out—that I am a monster. It feels like an eternity goes by. Maybe that's how much time passes. Who the hell knows?

Does time move differently here than in the human world? I'm not sure. I'm not sure about anything really, other than the few details Jude told me. This leaves me in a very vulnerable situation. I mean, if I knew more about my world and my powers, maybe I could figure out a way to get out of this cage. Or perhaps I should just stay in it. After all, Roman said the magic in the bars would only melt away if I wasn't evil.

If I am evil, maybe I should remain here where I can't hurt anyone else.

Still, as time ticks by, restlessness starts to stir inside me. I grow hungry. Frustrated.

I need to get out of here.

I eyeball the handheld device on the other side of the bars. Jude never mentioned what was on there, but if it works similar to human electronic devices, then maybe I can message him. Or search for ways to get out of this cage via the internet.

Wait ... Is there even internet here?

"Dammit, this is so frustrating," I mutter, keeping my attention on the handheld device.

While I'm not sure what it does exactly, right now, it's my best bet on getting out of here, since these bars show no signs of melting anytime soon.

Taking a deep breath, I lie flat on my stomach and stick

my arm through a gap between two bars. My fingers brush the device, and I start to—

The door to the dorm swings open, and I jerk back just as Roman, Ollie, and Phoenix stroll inside.

Roman's gaze immediately skates to the cage, and a trace of a smirk touches his lips. "Just as I expected."

I grit my teeth, glaring at him as I scoot back and lean against the bars. "Screw you."

Phoenix looks at me, his blood-stained lips tugging into a grin. "Yeah, we should definitely do that."

"I second that." Ollie grins as he shuts the door behind him.

"Watch it," Roman warns them as he makes his way over to a bar in the corner and begins to fix himself a drink of … Well, I'm not sure what the sparkling gold liquid is.

"Oh, come on, Rome," Ollie gripes as he joins Roman at the bar. Phoenix stays where he is, though, near my cage, watching me with his ruby eyes. "We can just let her out for a while, have some fun with her, and then put her back in the cage." His eyes light up. "She could be our pet. Our prisoner pet."

My heart rate quickens. *Pet? No effing way!* I've spent way too many years being controlled by people, and I refuse to do that again.

They can do anything they want with me, just like Tim did.

Phoenix's eyes flash bright red, almost like they're bleeding. "You guys are making her nervous," he remarks, his gaze never wavering from mine. It makes me nervous since he put me in a trance once, but I can't seem to look away. "Her pulse is soaring right now."

Take a deep breath, Haven. Calm down. Don't let them know you're afraid. Hold his gaze. Don't show weakness.

While I manage to carry his gaze, my pulse won't calm the hell down.

Phoenix's smirk magnifies. "Listen to her heart. It's pulsating, all that blood rushing under that pretty skin of hers." He sinks his fangs into his blood-stained lips. "She's afraid."

"He's right." Ollie collects a drink that Roman poured him and makes his way over to Phoenix, angling his head to the side. "But, why is she afraid?"

"I'm not positive, but we could always find out." Phoenix brushes a strand of his blue hair out of his eyes.

Ollie glances at him. "You wanna …?"

Phoenix shrugs, his eyes fixed on me. "It might not be a bad idea to see what's living in that dark mind of hers. We can find out what she's done in the past. Who she really is."

Ollie chews on his bottom lip, glancing at Phoenix. They exchange no words but turn simultaneously toward Roman.

"Rome, what do you think?" Ollie asks. "I mean, it'd take a lot of power, but we'd be able to get a good idea of what she's capable of."

Roman deliberately takes a sip of his drink, sets the

glass down on the counter, and then crosses his arms. "And then what? We know what she's done and keep her locked up? It seems completely pointless."

"Her being here isn't completely pointless," Phoenix tells him. "The academy doesn't let maddenings in. Not until her. And since we're …" He bites his bottom lip, stopping himself as Roman gives him a hard look. "Anyway, it might be a good idea to find out more about her. In doing so, maybe we can figure out why she's here."

"Plus, it wouldn't hurt to find out what she's capable of," Ollie adds, shoving up the sleeves of his shirt.

I realize two things then. One is that Roman almost seems like the leader of the three of them. And two being that they have some sort of secret. I'm not sure what, but I can tell by the hard look Roman gave Ollie right before he trailed off. I want to find out.

Roman remains silent, glancing from Ollie to Phoenix then to me. His dark eyes burrow into me and I want to look away, but again, I can't seem to.

"If we do this," he says, still looking at me but speaking to Ollie and Phoenix, "what're we going to do *when* we find out just how evil of a creature she is … how much death she's caused?"

His emphasis on *when* makes my jaw tick, like he thinks he knows me so well.

"I haven't killed anyone," I insist, kneeling up and gripping the bars, glaring at him. "You don't even know me, though you think you do."

Roman's gaze bores into me. "I may not know you now, but I will in a few minutes." He offers me a cruel smile that makes a chill seep into my bones.

"So, we're going to do it, then?" Phoenix asks Roman as he sits down on the edge of a table near the door.

Roman gives a calculating nod. "But, after we do, and we find out all the evil things she's done, we're going to throw her into The Cave of Doom."

I have no idea what The Cave of Doom is, but Ollie tenses, so I know it has to be bad. Which, I guess, is obvious since the title contains the word *doom*. It also lets me know that Ollie might be a *tiny* bit more sympathetic than the other two.

"That seems … I don't know, a little cruel," Ollie mutters then takes a sip of his drink.

Phoenix and Roman glance at Ollie, their brows arching.

"Is that hesitancy I sense?" Phoenix taunts, his lips curled into a smirk.

Ollie shakes his head. "No … Well … I don't know …" He blows out an exhale. "It just seems like such a waste to throw her in there without playing with her first."

Okay, maybe I was wrong about him being sympathetic.

I swallow hard then start racking my mind for a way

out of this, because I'm not doing this again. I refuse to be taunted. Abused. Broken by someone else. I could fight, but I'm not sure if my physical strength will stand up against theirs. As for my powers … yeah, I have no clue how to use them on cue. Plus, the idea of doing that to someone again …

I shudder as I recall the madness that took over Tim.

"Plus, you know I'm not a fan of that stupid cave," Ollie adds with a frown, setting his glass down on the table beside him.

Roman's and Phoenix's expressions soften ever so slightly and, for a moment, they don't look so scary.

"I know you're not a fan of it after what happened to Emilia," Roman tells him, his tone cautious, "but that cave will keep the maddening trapped there where she won't be able to hurt anyone."

They sink into silence, Roman and Phoenix staring at Ollie like they're worried he's about to break.

I make a mental note of that—that Ollie has a weakness. I'm guessing, Phoenix and Roman, too. If they have weaknesses, they can be broken.

Ollie rubs his lips together, contemplating. "All right, I guess I see your point." He picks up his glass again and downs the rest of the drink in one, long gulp.

He's nervous.

Good.

Maybe I can use that to my advantage, too.

Of course, when all three of them surround my cage, most of my confidence fizzles, unlike these stupid bars on this cage.

"Now we get to see all the evil that's living inside you," Roman tells me with a cold smile.

I force down a shaky breath. "What're you going to do?"

"Dig into your mind," Phoenix answers, flashing me his fangs as he raises his hands in front of him, "and look at all your memories so we can see all the horrible things you've done and use it against you."

No ... There's no way they can do that, right? Then again, I am sitting in a magical cage in an academy for monsters, so ...

Crap, what the heck am I going to do? Because the idea of them seeing some of the things that I've done, that have happened to me ...

No, I can't let this happen.

I need to get out of here.

I eye the handheld device, just out of my reach. If I can get to it, then maybe I can escape—

Knock. Knock. Knock.

The sound of someone knocking on the door has never sounded so lovely. I breathe out in relief. That is ... until none of them make any move to answer it.

"Just ignore it," Roman tells Ollie, glancing at the door with his hands in front of him, his palms shimmering with glittery light.

Shadows dance across his skin as Roman carries my gaze with pure hatred in his eyes, even though he doesn't even know me. He simply found out what I was and hated me because of it.

I decide right then and there that, if I end up getting out of this mess, I will hate him as much as he hates me.

I carry his gaze, hoping that hatred shines through—

Knock. Knock. Knock.

"Ollie," a female singsongs from the other side of the door. "I know you're in there, so open up, or I'll just burn the door down and kick your ass."

My eyes widen. *Burn the door down? Who the heck is on the other side of the door?*

"Dammit, Harper," Ollie mumbles under his breath, lowering his sparkling hands to his sides.

"Get rid of her," Roman hisses, crossing his arms.

"I'll try"—Ollie grimaces as he starts toward the door—"but you know how she can get sometimes."

"Personally, I'm glad she's here," Phoenix remarks with a grin.

Ollie blasts him with a glare. "How many times have I told you not to hit on my sister?"

Phoenix raises his hands in surrender, but a wicked smile remains on his lips. "Have I ever?"

"No." Ollie wraps his fingers around the door handle. "But everyone knows you have a thing for her."

Phoenix's smile dissipates. "I don't ever have a thing for anyone."

"Sure you don't," Roman mumbles with a roll of his eyes.

Phoenix glowers at Roman. "Since when do you take his side?"

"I never take anyone's side," Roman assures him, fiddling with a leather band on his wrist. "I'm just stating a fact, which is that you do have a thing for Harper."

"Whatever," Phoenix grumbles, his red eye dulling to a deep grey. "You guys don't know shit."

Neither one of them say anything else, but I detect an eye roll from Ollie before he opens the door. Then he positions himself in front of the opening so the girl on the other side can't see into the room—can't see me.

"What do you want?" Ollie aims for a firm tone but doesn't quite get there.

"Oh, don't try to take that attitude with me, twin brother," Ollie's sister—apparently twin sister—says. "We both know I'm more powerful than you, despite what you tell everyone. So, if I wanted to, I could totally magic fry your ass."

Ollie shakes his head then sighs. "Look, we're kind of busy right now, so do you need anything or not?"

"Actually, I have a very specific thing I need," she replies. "I'm looking for a girl, about our age. I'm not sure what she looks like, but she's a creature that rhymes with shmaddening."

My heart rate quickens, my full attention centering on that door. Phoenix's does, too. Roman, though, takes it one step further and strides over there, nudging Ollie out of the way.

"How did you find out about her?" he asks, or more like demands.

"Oh, Rome, how many times must I tell you that you can try to pull that alpha crap on me, but it'll never work." Her tone oozes sugary sweet sarcasm as she reaches forward and pats his cheek. "I know you way too well and can remember that sweet, little death angel that used to share all his toys in grade school."

Every single one of Roman's muscles tighten. "Watch it, Harper. You're about to cross a line."

"Again, I repeat: you don't scare me, death angel," she says.

Then Roman stumbles back, I'm assuming because she pushed him.

"Dude, Harper, what the hell is your problem?" Ollie shakes his head at the girl who strolls by a glaring Roman.

She looks similar to Ollie, with pale blonde hair, blue eyes, pointy ears—otherworldly beautiful. Her hair is a lot longer, though, flowing down her back, and she has a purple streak in the front. She's also a little bit shorter but still tall, and she's wearing a black dress, leather jacket, and platform shoes.

The moment she enters the room, her eyes land on me. "Aw, there she is." She smiles, but I can't tell if it's friendly or not.

"How did you know we had her?" Ollie inquires.

"Jude told me." Harper's heels click against the floor as she ambles toward me and crosses her arms, tilting her head to the side. "So, what sort of cage is this? A soul-stealing one? A mind-tormenting one?" She taps her fingers against her purple, shimmering lips. "No, wait. I bet it's an evil-capturing one?" She glances at Roman, Ollie, then Phoenix. "Am I right?"

"Yeah." Ollie appears guilty about it as he scratches the back of his neck. "But we're doing it for the benefit of everyone who goes to the academy—to protect everyone."

Harper dramatically rolls her eyes. "Don't try to pretend like you care about anyone in this school. I know you, Ollie, almost as well as I know myself, so I know that you don't care about anyone else in this school. Except for your little minions."

"Hey," Phoenix protests while Roman scowls at her.

"Watch it, Harper," Roman warns, moving away from the door and toward her.

Harper only rolls her eyes again. "Please, let's skip this bit again and get to the point of why I'm here, which is to collect the maddening from you guys."

Roman shakes his head. "We're not giving her to you."

"Oh, yes, you are," Harper tells him, folding her arms and staring him down.

The muscles in Roman's jaw pulsate. "We were instructed by Mor and Sage to guide her around the school and to let her live with us, so unless someone higher up gave you orders, you're not taking her."

"Oh, I know what your orders are," Harper informs him. "And let's not all pretend like there wasn't a very intentional purpose as to why a maddening ended up with you three."

No one says anything to that, leaving me to wonder what she means.

"So, here's what we're going to do," Harper continues. "You're going to let her out of the cage, she'll come stay with me in my dorm, and my friends and I will be her guide. If Mor and Sage check in, you three will do what you do best and lie to them. You'll tell them she's still living with you and that you're taking care of her."

Roman's shadowy gaze sears into her, but Harper seems completely unfazed.

"And why would we do that," he questions with a cock of his brow, "when we could just keep her here with us and do whatever we want with her?"

She offers him a cocky smile. "Because, if you don't let her come with me, I'll tell Charlie what you guys have planned for this year."

The shadows dancing across Roman's skin fade. "I don't know what you're talking about."

She pats his cheek. "Yes, you do, sweetheart."

He grits his teeth, his eyes full of shadowy fire as he glares at her then at me. "Fine," he bites out, tearing his gaze off me. Then he inches toward Harper, getting in her face, but she doesn't even so much as step back. "But whatever happens with her is on you."

She merely lifts a shoulder. "Fine by me."

Frustration seeps from Roman as he strides across the room and stops in front of the cage.

"You sure about this?" Phoenix asks Roman as moves up beside him.

"Do we have another choice?" Roman glances at him and arches his brow.

Phoenix rubs his lips together then shakes his head, grimacing. "I guess not."

"Okay, then." Roman looks back at me. Or, more like glares.

"Okay, then"—Ollie steps up beside the cage—"let's get her out of here." Unlike Phoenix and Roman, he seems more upbeat about the idea of giving me over to Harper. But that might just be due to the fact that he doesn't have to go to the Cave of Doom. Not that it matters.

No, what matters is that I'm getting out of this cage. Although, as the three of them lift their hands and emit sparks of magic at the bars while muttering incoherently under their breaths, I feel slightly disappointed for not being good enough to get rid of the bars myself. That doesn't mean that, as soon as the cage evaporates into thin air, I don't leap to my feet, rush out of the space, and grab my handheld device and bag.

"Smart choice, boys." Harper smirks at the three of them, and then her gaze falls on me. Unlike the death triplets, her eyes don't blaze with loathing.

I just hope it's not an act.

"Come on; let's get out of here," she tells me, nodding for me to follow her as she starts toward the door.

I slip on my backpack and hug my handheld device against my chest as I eagerly follow her.

Right as I'm about to step out of the room, Roman calls out, "This isn't over, maddening."

Although a chill slips across my skin, I glance at him with my brows lifted while slowly shutting the door behind me, silently saying: *Yes, it is.*

Of course, the moment the door shuts, reality bitch slaps me hard.

While I may have just escaped the death triplets, as long as I'm here, they can easily come after me again.

HAVEN

Harper says nothing after we exit the dorm room as she powerwalks down a wide, lantern-lit hallway, the floor paved with cobblestone. At first, I think she's not going to talk to me, that maybe her rescuing me was solely because Jude told her to. How did he even know I needed rescued?

"Okay." Harper suddenly slows her pace, letting an exhale ease from her lips. "I think we're in the clear now."

My boots scuff against the floor as I move up to walk beside her. "The clear of what?"

"Of them deciding to come after us," she clarifies, tucking a strand of hair behind her ear.

"You were worried they would?" I ask. "Because you seemed so confident they wouldn't."

She laughs, shaking her head. "Yeah, I totally faked it. Had to, or they'd destroy me." She loops her arm through mine, totally throwing me off. It's been a long time—okay, never—since anyone has just given me a friendly touch. "The thing with my brother and his friends is that they feed off people's fears. So, if you don't show them any fear, it not only throws them off, but it takes the fun out of their tormenting."

"Why are they like that?" I wonder, a thousand questions burning at the tip of my tongue.

"There are a lot of reasons," she tells me. "And honestly, I don't even know all of them. But the biggest one is death."

"Death?" Okay, that so wasn't what I thought she was going to say.

She nods, giving me a sidelong glance. "They used to be really sweet—my brother and his friends—but, when we were all around twelve or so, they all lost someone close to them. Ollie lost his friend, Emilia, in a tragic accident. Phoenix lost his mother. And Roman … he lost his brother. After that, they became … well, awful."

"Oh." I feel a bit of sympathy for them, and I'm not even sure why.

After what they just did to me, I should hate them, right? And I still do. But that doesn't mean I can't feel sorry for them, too.

While I've never met my parents, I've always felt the pain of not having them in my life.

Lonely.

Aching.

Broken.

That's how I feel when I think about them.

"Anyway"—she tugs me to the right as the hallway splits into a fork—"I'm just glad I got there before they ended up doing something irreversible to you."

"Me, too," I agree then pause, wondering how much to tell her. I mean, I have no clue why Jude sent her to get me, unless he somehow knew the death triplets would do what they did to me. "They were going to take me to the Cave of Doom ... whatever that is."

Her eyes widen as her gaze darts to me. "Seriously?"

"That's what they said."

"I can't believe it," she mutters in astonishment.

I'm not sure why she's so shocked. After all, she basically told me the death triplets are awful.

"After what happened to Emilia ..." She shakes her head repeatedly, anger biting in her expression. "I can't believe Ollie would even consider doing that to anyone."

"Well, he did protest about it for a bit," I tell her.

"Still ..." She shakes her head again then sighs. "Well, I'm glad I got there in time."

"Me, too," I agree again. "But, why did you show up? Not that I'm not grateful. Just ... how did you know about me and that I'd need help?"

She makes another turn as the hallway splits again. At this point, I'm starting to worry that I'll never be able to find my way around this place. There are so many twists and turns, and all the hallways look similar. Well, except this one is lined with red doors.

"Jude came to me right after he left you in their dorm," she explains, eyeing the silver numbers on the doors. "He knew it was a bad idea for you to be left with them. He also knew that, if he tried to get you out of there himself, he'd not only get fired, but my brother and his minions would torment him."

"How can they do that?" I wonder. "Isn't he an authority figure around here?" Or maybe there are no authority figures here. I'm not sure how that works in a monster school.

"He technically is," she tells me, coming to a stop in front of a door. I realize then that there are no doorknobs or locks on it, or any of the other doors. "However, my family, Roman's, and Phoenix's donate enough money to this school that we can get away with almost anything." She places her hand against the door. "So, that's why Jude came to me. He knew I could get away with taking you and that the death triplets would more than likely not do anything to me."

"More than likely?" I question. "You weren't one-hundred percent sure?"

She gives me a look of pity. "Jude told me that you just learned of this world and your powers, so I'm going to tell you something very important about magic and monsters and this magical world you're now going to call your home. Nothing about anything is one hundred percent. Nothing is certain. Remember that, and you should be okay here." She then looks at the door and whispers, "*Ego sum dominus huius cubiculum. Aperta.*" As the door clicks open, she lowers her hand and looks at me. "And remember *that* if you want to be able to get into your new room." With that, she pushes open the door and steps inside.

While part of me wants to run and pretend none of this ever happened, the other part of me knows I have nowhere to go. So, taking a deep breath, I follow her into the room that I'm supposed to call my home for the next year.

HAVEN

THE ROOM ENDS UP BEING SIMILAR TO THE DEATH TRIPLETS'. Only, the velvet couches are black, more mirrors hang on the walls, and there's no bar but a massive vanity with several jewel-decorated chairs.

"You can take the room on the right," Harper tells me, pointing to one of the four, arched doorways. Then she shucks off her jacket, tosses it onto the back of the sofa, and makes her way over to a kitchen area in the far left corner. "Our other roommates won't be here for another week. We're actually here pretty early, but I always come early." She pauses, glancing at me. "Jude never mentioned why you showed up earlier."

I'm not sure what to tell her. Jude was very specific about creatures not knowing what I was, yet the death triplets know, and Harper. And we never came up with a story of what to say to creatures about what I am.

I part my lips, about to tell her that I have no idea why I arrived early, when someone knocks on the door.

Harper holds up a finger. "Hold that thought." Then she whisks across the room, scooping up a … stick from off the table.

When she notices me staring at it, she grins. "It's my wand."

"Oh." So wands exists. And faeries use them?

How does that even work? I always thought only witches used wands.

"I can tell you have a crap ton of questions," Harper says, clutching her wand. "And I'll totally get around to answering them, but first, I need to answer the door. And I want to be careful, because I'm mildly concerned my brother and his minions may have changed their minds about making this easy on us."

I stiffen as she grips the door handle, yanks open the door, and points the wand at …

Jude.

His flaming eyes widen as he hurriedly raises his hands. "Easy, Harper, it's just me."

Harper exhales in relief as she lowers her wand. "Sorry. I was just a little bit worried my brother and his stupid friends decided to retaliate already."

"Already?" I'm not sure why I'm surprised. Roman made it pretty clear this wasn't over yet.

At the sound of my voice, Jude's gaze finds me, and smoke washes across his face, the flames fizzling. "Oh, good, you're here, which means my plan worked." He steps inside, and Harper shuts the door behind him. "I'm sorry I had to bail on you, but I had to play this right, or there'd be consequences."

"It's fine. Harper explained why you had to do what you did." I chew on my bottom lip. "I am a little confused, though, about why you helped me at all. I mean, why would you risk your job when you don't even know me?"

Pity flickers in his eyes as he stops in front of me. "Because I know what it feels like to be bullied, and I never want anyone to have to go through that."

"Oh." I don't know what to say to that. Part of me wants to hug him, but I've never really hugged anyone, let alone a fire demon, so I'm not really sure if it'd be weird. Plus, wouldn't I start on fire or something?

"Anyway ..." Jude clears his throat. "Now that we have you out of that situation, we have one week to prepare you for when all the other students arrive. Harper is going to be your guide. She'll teach you everything you need to know about the academy. It also means she'll need to know your backstory. But it's okay; you can trust her."

I wonder how he knows that for sure.

As if sensing my doubt, Harper wanders over to us and

says, "Jude and I did a blood promise that swears me to secrecy." She sets the wand down on an ebony end table. "And, since I'm fairly sure you don't know what that is, you should know that that kind of a promise isn't breakable. The magic that seals it won't allow me to break it."

I give an uneven nod, feeling a bit overwhelmed. "Okay."

"Okay, then." Jude claps his hands together. "Should we get to it?" He looks from me to Harper. "I'm thinking we should start on the history of the school and go from there."

"Do we really have to cover that?" Harper asks with a grimace. "I mean, they'll cover that in Ancient History of the Academy, which she'll have to take since she's starting out as a freshman."

"Yeah, but I want her to have a little bit of knowledge." Jude snaps his fingers, and a handheld device appears in his hand. "Not going in completely blind might be the thing that saves her from this ending in a disaster."

Harper glances at me then nods. "Maybe you're right."

While I'm grateful they're helping me out, I'm left wondering how they expect this to end.

Just what sort of disaster is heading my way?

For the next several hours, Jude, Harper, and I sit on the sofas as Jude explains the history of the school. And, while I try to latch on to every detail, I quickly learn why Harper was so hesitant about Jude teaching me about the history of the academy.

It's boring. And honestly, kind of annoying.

I mean, ordinarily, it was created to train talented monsters with magical powers to become hunters and huntresses, which are monsters who spend their lives devoted to tracking evil monsters down, like the witch that shoved me into the portal that led me here. The problem is that, over the years, the academy struggled with getting finances because, apparently, the monster government—yeah, that's a thing—didn't want to support the cause. Their reason was because they believed it was unnecessary, that the government should oversee the imprisonment of creatures. But, at least according to Jude, that system was totally corrupt. Creatures were bought off, evil prevailed, and so the academy was created. But, without funding, hardly anyone wanted to attend due to the lack of good teachers and living quarters. And so, they started recruiting wealthy families to donate to the cause, which led to corruptness in the school. Like, for example, the fact that the death triplets can do whatever they want without any repercussions.

"This school is very political," Harper explains as she nibbles on a bowl of strawberries that she retrieved from the fridge about half an hour ago.

She offered to get me something to eat when she went to get them but, at the time, I wasn't sure what faeries ate, so I declined her offer. Now, my mouth is salivating with hunger.

When was the last time I ate anything?

Better yet, how much time has gone by since I got here?

"That it is," Jude agrees, setting his handheld device down on his lap. "And this school has become an academy mostly for the wealthy, though there are scholarship students, which is what you're going to be." He glances down at the screen of the handheld device. "The problem is that all scholarship students come here because they've gotten sponsorship. And the groups and creatures that sponsorship students make their choices based on the creature's grades, school performance, and talent. However, you come from the human world, so you have no talent yet, and your grades and performance are … Well, I think, in the human world, they just grade you on your ability to memorize facts." His gaze lifts to mine. "Am I correct?"

I waver. "Kind of."

"Hmm …" He thrums his finger against his lips. "So that leaves us with very little options."

"Do I really need a sponsorship?" I ask. "I mean, I have clothes already." I pat my backpack that's next to me on the sofa. "And, other than food, I don't really need anything else."

For like the tenth time since we met, pity fills Jude's expression. "Oh, sweetie."

"What?" I wonder.

He just trades a worried look with Harper. "This might be harder than we thought."

"Perhaps," Harper agrees, assessing me closely. "But not completely undoable."

Again, I'm perplexed. "What is?"

Jude exhales a weary sigh. "Getting you to blend in." He tosses the handheld device onto the cushion beside him. "We need that in order for you not to get too many eyes on you, which we don't want if we want to keep your identity hidden."

My lips form an O as worry stirs through me.

Harper observes me for a beat or two longer before she

sits up straighter. "I'll get her there," she assures Jude. "You find a way to get her a sponsorship."

"And how do you propose I do that?" Jude questions. "We have only a week left before classes start."

Harper shrugs. "I don't know. Find someone who wants to sponsor an orphan. I mean, there has to be a creature out there who will take pity on her."

Smokes hiss from Jude's hair as he wavers his head from side to side. "I might have an idea …" He picks up his handheld device, drifts from the sofa, and strides toward the door. "I'll be in touch," he mutters as he pulls open the door.

Before he walks out of the room, he casts a glance over his shoulder at me. "There's an app on your handheld device that works a lot like texting. Have Harper show you how to use it and feel free to message me at any time."

He looks at Harper. "Please take care of her until I get back. I'll be back tomorrow night."

Harper gives him a salute.

Smoke wisps out of Jude's lips as he blows out a breath then exits the room, shutting the door behind him.

Once he's gone, Harper twists to face me. "Thank God he came up with an idea for a sponsor."

I nod in agreement. "I'm glad, too. Although, I'm still not sure why I need one."

"Trust me; you need one," she stresses, popping another strawberry into her mouth. "But that's not the only reason why I'm glad he got an idea for one." She sticks the bowl of strawberries in my direction, offering me one.

I eagerly accept, grabbing a couple and stuffing them into my mouth. "What's the other reason?" Good God, these might be the best strawberries I've ever had. Well, either that or I'm starving.

She grins. "So we don't have to listen to anymore of his boring stories about the academy's history. I seriously fell asleep with my eyes open."

A laugh escapes me. The sound is startling.

It's been a very long time since I laughed. In fact, I can't even remember the last time I have.

In that moment, I feel like perhaps maybe everything will be okay.

It's a naïve thought, something I learn with time.

HAVEN

HARPER AND I SPEND THE REST OF THE DAY GETTING SETTLED in, since she hasn't unpacked. She has five suitcases and a large trunk to unpack, so it takes her much longer than me. In fact, it takes me a whopping five minutes to stuff my few worn outfits into one of three dressers lining the lavender walls of my spacious room.

Don't even get me started on the walk-in closet. Bigger than most of the rooms I've stayed in and lined top to bottom with shelves. My pair of sneakers look awfully lonely perched by themselves.

I slip off my jacket and hang it up, trying to help the emptiness, but it somehow makes the scene even more pathetic.

Honestly, I feel pathetic just standing in the massive room beneath the black diamond, shimmering chandelier, surrounded by ebony dressers, a gigantic four-poster bed, and shiny marble floors. The ceiling is domed and painted with an array of purple and black tinted colors that form shapes and swirls of a land that sparkles with magic, one I kind of wish I could see.

"You seem stunned?" Harper remarks, appearing in the doorway. She's changed into a pair of black pajama bottoms, a striped shirt, and her hair is now pulled up into a high ponytail.

Is it bed time already? What time is it? I still haven't figured out the whole time thing. I looked on the handheld deceive for a clock, but all I could find was some weird-ass compass-looking thing.

I twist to face her. "Honestly, I kind of am." I fiddle with a tiny hole in the hem of my shirt. "I'm not used to having my own room, let alone one this big and fancy."

Even when I was at Tim and Tina's as the only foster kid, I slept on the sofa. They had an extra room, and they told the social workers that's where I would stay, but then, once they were gone, Tina insisted she needed it for storage, so I had to sleep on the sofa.

"That's really sad," she tells me. "I've heard stories about the human world. That it's kind of horrible there."

I want to tell her it's not bad, but … "I think it's probably not awful for everyone. Since I don't have a family, though, I only had temporary ones. In the foster system … Do you guys have that here?" I ask, and she shakes her head with a crease between her brows. "Well, it's basically a system for kids who don't have parents. You get placed with temporary ones, and there's usually more than one foster kid living there, so things can get sort of cramped."

The crease between her brow deepens. "Why don't they just find you a permanent home and family?"

"Some kids do," I explain, wrapping my arms around myself. "But for some kids … like me … We never do get a place we call home. Or a family …" As pain swells inside me, I clear my throat. "Anyway, yeah, that's why I've never had my own room."

She hesitates before stepping through the doorway and into the room. "How did you never know you had powers? Did they never manifest? Or did you just not realize what was going on?"

I sink my teeth into my lip. This is a tough subject for me.

"Sorry. You don't have to tell me if you don't want to," she quickly adds. "I'm just trying to learn more about you."

"It's just a little weird talking about it," I admit. "My powers have only manifest two times, and both times were"—I swallow hard—"awful. I didn't know what was going on. Honestly, I thought … well, I thought I was crazy."

"Which is kind of ironic, considering what you can do." A joking smile turns at her lips.

I could get offended, but I find myself smiling instead. "Yeah, it kind of is."

Her smile widens. "You know what, Haven? I think you and I are going to become good friends."

I want to ask her if it'll be a real friendship or if it'll be pretend, like everything else about my life. I want to ask her why she's doing this. If she's afraid of me. I want to ask her a lot of questions, but I worry the answers might break me. So, I keep smiling and pretending this is all real instead.

Maybe it isn't, though.

Maybe, one day, I'll wake up and be back in the human world. Maybe this is all a nightmare. Or a dream. I haven't really decided yet how I feel about everything.

She claps her hands together and smiles, drawing me from my thoughts. "Okay, so what I'm thinking is that, tomorrow, I can give you the tour of the school, which yes, will probably take all day."

My jaw nearly hits the marble floor. "It's that big?"

She nods. "Yep. And trust me; if you're out of shape, your legs are going to get so sore."

I pull a face. "I'm pretty out of shape."

She considers this. "Me, too. Maybe we should take a yoga class or something."

"Monsters do yoga?"

"Yeah ... Why wouldn't we?" She looks at me like I'm insane.

Maybe I am.

"I just thought yoga was a human thing."

"Hey, monsters have to exercise, too. And I usually try to stay in better shape over the summer so I can kick ass in The Deadly Trials, but I let myself become stupidly distracted by a guy. Word of advice: never date an ogre." She roams around my room, peeking in my closet and frowning.

"I won't," I assure her, trying to picture her dating one.

From what I've seen in books, ogres are hideous creatures with warts and bulky body parts.

"You look confused," she muses. "That's okay. So am I."

"Sorry, it's just that I'm trying to picture you dating an ogre, and I can't … Wait—why are you confused?"

"Because there's literally two things in your closet." She points over her shoulder at the closet. "Why are you confused about me dating an ogre?"

"Aren't they supposed to be … I don't know, like wart-y?" As soon as the words leave my lips, I realize how shallow I sound.

Looks should not matter, Haven.

She snorts a laugh. "You, best friend, have a very misconstrued idea of what an ogre is."

"So they're not wart-y?"

"Gods, no. They're gorgeous. Almost too gorgeous."

"Oh." My thoughts drift to the death triplets and how beautiful they are.

I wonder if ogres are more gorgeous than them? Is that even possible? Not that that means anything. They may be gorgeous, but they're total assholes. Dangerous, deadly assholes who know what I am …

A thought occurs to me then. One that makes my stomach churn with anxiety.

"If the death triplets know what I am, shouldn't I be worried they'll tell everyone?" I ask.

She shakes her head without missing a beat. "Mor and Sage made them take a blood promise before they even told them about you. At least, that's what Jude said. And Jude isn't much of a liar."

Relief trickles through me. "That's good. How do you know Jude, anyway?"

She smiles as she walks back to me. "He was a third year when I started here, and I kind of had a crush on him. Unfortunately, my family never would've approved of him since he was a scholarship student." She rolls her eyes. "My family is full of some of the most pretentious creatures. Anyway, yeah, even though I couldn't act on my crush with Jude, we became friends."

I try to imagine her and Jude dating, with his fiery lips and flaming skin. "How would you not get burned? I mean, if you dated him and tried to touch him?"

"Oh, fire demons won't burn you unless they want to," she informs me. "The flames on his skin kind of feel like …

drinking faerie wine." A wistful look flashes across her face.

"I wouldn't know what that feels like since I've never touched a fire demon or drank faerie wine," I admit, feeling completely out of my element.

Story of my pathetic life.

"That's right. You probably haven't done much of anything," she states, seeming amused by this. "Well, magical things, anyway. What about human things? They have regular wine, right?" she asks, and I nod. "Have you ever tried that?"

I shake my head. "I haven't done much of anything."

"What about kissing?" she continues on, appearing totally entertained by my lack of experiences. "Have you kissed anyone?"

Again, I shake my head. "No." Not of my own free will, anyway, but I'm not about to admit that aloud.

Her smile turns gleeful as she taps her fingers together. "We're so going to change that. Over the next year, you'll drink faerie wine, smoke magic, dance, party, and kiss so many guys you'll forget what kissing is like." She pauses. "Unless you're into girls. Or both. Either way, you'll get a lot of kissing done; trust me." Her confidence in the fact that it's going to be like that confuses the hell out of me.

"I'm not sure it'll be that easy." I sink down onto the foot of the bed and pick at a loose thread hanging from my shorts. "Guys generally don't given me the time of day. Plus, I'm beyond awkward."

"Awkward can be cute," she assures me. "And, if guys haven't given you the time of day, then human guys are way too sane. Trust me, though; monsters are much insane, and I have a feeling, when they see the new girl, they'll lose their minds even more."

Her sentence is so backward that it takes me a moment to process. And when I do, I want to change the subject immediately. Not just because I don't believe her, but even if it were true, even if some guys wanted me, I'm not sure I could ever be able to go there, to let anyone touch me without thinking of all the times I've been touched when I didn't want to be …

"How many different creatures go here?" I wonder, changing the subject. "This is an academy for monsters, so how many types are there?"

"Oh, there's way more than you'll be able to count, and probably a ton you've never heard of. I'll try to point them out on the first day. Honestly, I don't even know all the different species." As I start to feel overwhelmed, she adds, "Don't worry about all that just yet. For now, we're going to focus on coming up with your story and showing you around the school. Everything else will be a learn as you go sort of process."

She makes it sound so easy. I just hope she's right.

So far, everything about my life has been the opposite.

HAVEN

I HAVE TO ADMIT THAT, DESPITE THE FACT THAT I SPENT THE night at an academy for monsters, I slept better than I ever have. Maybe it's because the bed is massive and the mattress is the most comfortable thing I've ever lain on. Or maybe it's because I was so damn exhausted from yesterday's events that the moment my head hit the pillow, I crashed. Whatever the reason, I feel oddly refreshed when I open my eyes. However, it takes me a moment to remember where I am, remember all the craziness that was yesterday. Once my mind settles into the fact, I sit up and rub my eyes with the heels of my hands, trying to rub the sleepiness from my eyes.

I'm about to climb out of bed when the handheld device Jude gave me yesterday buzzes from the nightstand.

I pick it up and tap the screen a few times, but nothing

happens. Then I scratch my head, wondering how this thing works. It looks like it should work like a human handheld device, but either the screen is busted or it clearly doesn't work that way.

"You have to use magic to unlock it," Harper informs me as she materializes in the doorway. And when I say materialize, I mean she appears out of thin air.

"How did you do that?" I ask in awe.

She's still in her pajamas, but her hair is down and strands fall into her eyes as she angles her head to the side. "Do what?"

"Appear out of thin air like that."

"Oh, that." She dismisses me with a flick of her wrist. "That's simple teleportation magic. About half the creatures can do it ... I don't think maddenings can, though."

"What ...?" I pause, nervous to ask, but knowing I need to find out. "Besides causing madness and ... death, is there anything else a maddening can do? Maybe something that's not so ... bad?"

Sympathy shimmers in her eyes. "I'm not sure. We don't really learn much about maddenings around here, since none have ever been allowed at the school. Well, except now, with you. But"—she wavers her head from side to side —"during our tour today, we can stop by the library and see what we can find out. We'll have to be careful about it, because we don't want anyone finding out what you are. Plus, more than likely, the info will be in The Deadly and

Forbidden Room, which is in the locked section of the library where they keep all the books that have dangerous and forbidden information in them."

Why is everything in this place labeled with *deadly* or *forbidden*?

"Then, how do we get in?"

She grins. "Didn't you just see how I arrived here?"

"Right," I say, still struggling to catch on to this whole magic thing.

"Oh, and I brought you breakfast." She grabs a bag seemingly out of nowhere and tosses it to me. "I'm going to get dressed. I'll be ready in about one to two compass rotations. Does that work for you?"

"Compass rotations?" I ask, picking up the bag she tossed at me.

She gives me a puzzled look before realization sweeps across her expression. "Right. Humans do the whole time thing differently, with the sun and moon, I think. Anyway …" She whisks over and sits down on the edge of the bed. "Put your palm to the device, shut your eyes, and think *unlock.*"

"Okay." Hesitation fills my tone as I place my palm on the screen and do what she instructed.

At first, nothing happens, but then I feel this warmth, this wonderful, sparkling iridescent warmth that radiates from my skin. And just like that, the screen of the handheld device lights up.

"Interesting," she murmurs as she glances at my arms.

"Is something wrong?" I ask worriedly.

She bites her bottom lip and shakes her head, her gaze lifting to mine. "It's just that your magic was iridescent."

I glance down at my arms as the iridescent glow fades. "Is that a bad thing?"

"No, but it's not a maddening thing, either. They're power is usually red or black." She mulls over something deeply. "Have you actually ever used your maddening powers before?"

My insides tremble as I recall the times that I have. "Yes. A couple of times, by accident." My tone quivers as I admit this, admit that I am a monster.

Her expression softens, and she gives my hand a sympathetic pat. "It's okay. Whatever happened, it wasn't your fault."

I wish I believed her, but part of me doesn't. Yet, I nod.

Silence stretches between us. I'm not sure what to say. Fortunately, my handheld device buzzes again.

"You've got a message," she announces, practically latching on to the distraction. "I'll show you how to check it in just a minute. Let me show you really quickly how to tell time here." She scoots closer and taps a compass app on the screen. "See the north, south, east, and west?" she asks, skimming her fingers along the compass.

I nod. "Yeah."

"Well, every time the arrow goes around once, it measures an hour."

"Okay …"

"You seem confused."

"It's just that compasses in the human world just show the direction you're standing in."

"Well, this does show the direction," she explains. "It's just the direction of our world in position to the starlight."

Again, I'm confused. Honestly, it's all I've really been since I got here. "Starlight?"

"Yeah, it's kind of like our sun. Although, it doesn't look similar. We'll have to go outside soon so I can show you." She stands. "Anyway, I'm going to go get cleaned up. I'll meet up with you when the compass returns to the north." She exits the room, a strange trail of silvery mist trailing behind her.

So strange.

Then again, magic just sparkled through me, so …

Shaking my head, I focus on the handheld device. Now that I've gotten the screen unlocked, I can see that it is a lot like a human phone, only the icons are much more eccentric. Like the message app, which is a werewolf spitting out an envelope. I find myself giggling softly at that as I tap on it.

I have two messages, both from Jude. One is to check in and make sure I'm okay, which I reply to with a yes. The other is a bit longer.

Haven,

I hope all is going well. I am still searching for a sponsor for you. Last night, I wanted to give you a brief rundown of your cover story that I came up with and Mor gave his approval of.

Your name will remain the same. You're also supposed to tell everyone you're a firelight witch, which are the most basic witches. You should be able to do most of what they do after a little bit of training that myself and Harper will give you.

These types of witches also have no distinct physical features, appearing merely human, so you won't have to try to alter your appearance. It is kind of rare that one gets accepted to the academy since their powers are fairly average, but you are to tell everyone that you ended up here because a sponsor took pity on you. Until I find you a sponsor, though, you're supposed to be very vague about who it is. Everything else about your story will remain similar to your actual story: you're an orphan, have little knowledge about who you are, and you haven't been taught to use your powers properly, which will help you if you get asked to use your powers and you can't yet. Unfortunately, this will get you put in a lot of lower level classes. For now, that's probably for the best.

Oh yes, and I've also forward this message to Harper.

See you soon,

Jude

After I read the message, I set the handheld device down and process everything I just read. Nothing about what was in the letter really bothered me, except the part where my past will remain similar to what it really is. Maybe it's stupid, but I think I secretly hoped I'd somehow not have to play the part of an orphan anymore. I guess it doesn't really matter. My cover story can't erase my real past.

Sighing quietly at that, I move on to getting ready, starting with eating breakfast. I'll admit, I'm a little apprehensive about opening up the bag Harper gave me. When I do, though …

"Wow." I take out a warm, blueberry muffin, a container of eggs, a few slices of sausage, a bowl of strawberries, and a jug of orange juice.

Normally, I just eat oatmeal or cereal for breakfast, so this might actually be the best breakfast I have ever had.

Excited, I dive in, practically stuffing every last drop of food into my mouth. When I'm finished, I down the orange juice, which has sort of a bubbly taste to it, but I figure that's probably just because I'm in some magical monster world.

"Holy crap," I mutter as reality kisses me on the cheek.

I'm in a magical world.

I'm magical.

Holy freakin' unicorns!

AFTER I EAT, I GET DRESSED AND MEET HARPER IN THE living room. Then we set out on our tour.

I'm feeling pretty dang good. Light even. I'm not positive why, other than maybe this place is starting to wear on me.

As Harper and I wander down the hallways, I keep getting distracted by everything—the way the lanterns sparkle, the dark colors splattered everywhere, and the various scents lacing the air. I'm really struggling to pay attention, but I try my best and manage to retain a little bit of information that Harper's telling me, not only about the academy but herself, as well.

"How old are you, anyway?" I ask when she tells me that monsters age differently.

"I'm seventeen," she replies. "For now, I'll age normally. But in a couple of years, it'll slow down drastically. Vampires are that way, too. So are pixies, angels … Honestly, most monsters either age very slowly or are immortal."

I twirl a strand of my hair around my finger. "What about maddenings?"

Her brows dip as she glances at me. "You know what? I think they are. We can double-check when we get to the library."

Immortality.

I …

I have no idea how to even process that.

I untangle my finger from my hair, my head spinning. "So, you're immortal, a dark faerie. What else do I need to know about you?"

"Well, my last name is Evenlee, which might not seem important, but it is. I come from a very powerful line of dark faeries, and all I have to do is say my last name and can practically get away with anything. Although that does have some downfalls, like certain expectations that come with it."

"What sort of expectations?"

She lifts a shoulder. "The biggest one is that I'm already betrothed to marry some prince I've never met."

My eyes widen. "What?"

"It's not that uncommon as you think. However, it totally sucks." A sad sigh escapes her lips. "The moment I graduate, I'm going to be shipped off to my husband-to-be. The only reason I was even allowed to attend here is because Ollie is my twin and we're stronger when we're closer. So, in order for him to graduate from this place at the top of our class, I needed to attend, too, so he could reach his top potential." She pulls a face at that.

So do I. "It kind of sounds sexist."

"It does, but it's not. There're male faeries that are in the same position as me."

"Are faeries the only creatures that do that?"

She shakes her head, laughing. "Not at all. A lot of creatures have arranged marriages or mates. Or, in death angel cases, wing matches. They're the only ones that have that."

"What is that?" I wonder, my gaze straying to a set of tall doors just down the hallway.

"It's kind of like a soulmate. Except, when a death angel finds their wing match, they can combine their powers and become super powerful," she explains. "I think it has to do with their feathers being laced with magic belonging to the same wing weaver."

I gape at her. "I don't … I literally have no clue what most of that meant."

She smiles encouragingly. "You'll get there. It'll take some time, but you will."

I hope so, because the last thing I want is to walk around feeling as clueless and as stupid as I do now.

"I know something that might make you feel a little bit better about all this," she tells me suddenly. "At least about what you are. It has to do with where dark faeries' bloodlines come from." She takes a deep breath. "Our magic derives from a demon bloodline, unlike other faeries, whose magic comes from the land and the faerie gods."

I may have freaked out at the word demon, but considering what Jude told me what maddenings can do and that Jude is a fire demon, it doesn't even faze me.

In fact, I've felt strangely calm all afternoon.

Maybe it's this place. Or knowing what I am. Or maybe it's that, for the first time in like forever, someone is being nice to me.

"You don't need to be afraid of me," Harper says quietly, misreading my silence. "Unless a dark faerie wants to be evil, they don't have to be."

"Why would I be afraid of you if you're not of me?" I point out as my gaze skims the painted ceiling. "That would just make me a total hypocrite."

I've noticed that each hallway's ceiling is painted differently. This one has a mural of what looks like a crystalized lake. Harper told me that all the places painted around the school exist, but most you have to portal travel to, which yeah, that took me a moment to take in …

"It's just kind of a habit for me to think that. Usually, when creatures hear what I am, they freak out." She studies me with a small smile. "I forgot you're different, though."

Am I? Even in a world full of monsters?

"Well, you don't have to be afraid of me, either," I try to assure her, hoping I'm telling the truth. I want to be, but the two times I've used my powers, I've ended up hurting someone. It makes me wonder how I'll ever learn to control them if no one knows I'm a maddening.

What the heck am I going to learn here?

"I know I don't need to be afraid of you," she assures me, gathering her hair into a ponytail. Then she lowers her hands from her hair, not securing it with an elastic, yet the ponytail stays there.

It has to be because of magic.

"How do you know, though?" I wonder.

"Because I can just tell." She doesn't embellish, slowing to a stop in front of a set of plain double doors. "Okay, so, returning back to the tour for a moment." She gestures at the double doors. "This is the cafeteria where we eat in a land full of drama. Seriously, I'm not sure what lunchtime at human schools are like, but here, it's all about cliques."

"It's the same there, too. Although, I was never in a clique. I was kind of a loner."

"Well, you won't be one here, because you're going to be part of my clique."

I appreciate that, I really do, but part of me wonders if she's being my friend because she wants to be or because Jude asked her to. Not that I'm going to stop being her friend because of that. Favor or not, it's nice not to have to be a loner anymore.

"The rest of my clique are my roommates. Well, except for Eva.'" She pulls a face at that. "I don't even know how she got put into our dorm this year, but it's going to suck if we can't get her to transfer to another one. And if that happens, it'll be just you, me, Remi, and Atashia. And they're all really cool."

"Okay," I say. "But, why is Eva so bad?"

"Because she's a bitch, plain and simple. And she's been my and my friends' archenemy for years now. Honestly, I think she may have purposely got put in our dorm just so she can torment us." She shakes her head in annoyance. "Her parents are the most powerful pixies to ever exist, and they're friends with Mor, so all she has to do is snap her finger and she gets what she wants." She points a finger at me. "And you need to be extra careful around her. She's going to want to come after you."

I point at myself. "Me? Why the hell for?"

"Because you're pretty," she replies simply. "And a scholarship student. And an average witch. The prettiness, she'll be jealous of, and the rest, she'll see as a weakness, so you'll be the perfect target." She briefly pauses, a hint of worry transpiring in her eyes. "And I hate to say this, but I feel like I need to. She probably won't be the only creature that will want to torment you because of all those traits."

Awesome. I guess, even in the monster world, I'm going to be a loser.

"Don't worry; me and my friends will have your back," she promises, her lips curving into a grin. "And trust me; we're pretty badass."

"I remember," I tell her, recalling how she basically took me from the death triplets without so much as making a drop of magic sizzle from her fingers.

"Good." She continues to smile as she moves to the next door. "Okay, so this is the storage closet …" She trails off. "For the love of all boring pixies, this tour is boring."

"Sorry," I apologize since the only reason she has to do this is because of me.

She elevates her brows at me. "Why are you apologizing? You're not the one giving this boring-ass tour."

"But you only have to do it because of me," I point out, tucking a loose strand of hair behind my ear.

"Yeah, so? I've got nothing better to do." She gives a simple shrug.

I'm not sure if she's being truthful or not, since I'm still trying to figure her out. She's very sarcastic—that much I've picked up on. She also likes to dress in black. Right now, she's rocking a pair of black pants, a matching tank top, and knee-high purple boots. I have on a black tank top, too, along with the shorts I had on yesterday, but I pulled on a plaid shirt to cover up the old ranch dressing stain that's on the side of my tank top. And, while her hair flows down her back in perfect curls, mine is swept to the side in a tangled mess. Part of me envies her put-together-ness, but the other part of me knows I'll always be a hot mess and should just own it.

"What we need to do is mix things up. Make this tour a lot more interesting." She taps her finger against her shimmering, iridescent lips. The color isn't from lipstick, but from magic, something she informed me of when I asked her about it this morning. "Oh." Her eyes light up. "I can show you the auditorium where the deadly games take place."

She mentioned the deadly games yesterday, but I was too distracted by the immense load of other information being thrown at me to ask what it is. Now I'm dying to know.

No pun intended.

"What is the deadly games, anyway?" I ask as I trail after her down the hallway.

"It's an event that happens at the beginning of October to represent sponsor month," she explains, slowing to a halt in front of two, lofty, steel doors with curling handles and eyes carved into them. "The games are a way to pay back all the sponsors who donate to this school by giving them a little bit of entertainment."

"What sort of entertainment?" I ask as she grips the door handles. "Because the title of the game sounds very … ominous."

"That's because it is." The doors let out the most ear-splitting creak as she pulls them open. "You're dealing with a whole new world, Haven Wyllowravelee. One where danger lurks everywhere. Not that I want to scare the crap out of you, but you also need to know the truth, or you won't survive." She tentatively steps into the auditorium, and I follow, my jaw nearly cracking against the ash-stained floor. "And the truth is this is a dangerous, dangerous place."

My eyes roam around the metal spikes covering the concrete walls, the oily black ceiling and the chains dangling from them, and the archways all over the place that seem to lead to darkness. Running along the upper section of the walls are rows and rows of thrones perched on glass platforms.

"I don't understand." I force my gaze from what looks like a torture chamber. "If this academy is so dangerous, why does anyone go here?"

An ominous look crosses her face. "Because the worlds are a much more dangerous place than here. Way more dangerous."

Maybe she's right. After all, I spent most of my life being mocked, abused, touched, beaten, and tormented by humans. But this room …

"What exactly happens in this room?" I dare ask. "I mean, what are the deadly games?"

Her gaze travels to the room, fear fleetingly flashing in her eyes, but the look dissipates as she glances back at me. "Come on; let's finish the tour, and I'll explain on the way."

We leave the room, closing the door behind us, and I become aware of how cold the space had been, as if the air had been sucked dry of the warmth.

"So, the deadly games … where to start?" She wavers her head from side to side as we lollygag up the hallway. "Well, like I said, the games happen at the beginning of October, but the participants get picked at the start of the school year by random selection. There are a lot of schools that compete."

"Wait … This isn't the only monster academy?"

"Nope. This one only specializes in training hunters and huntresses. There're also ones that focus on government skills, creation of worlds, world domination—stuff like that."

My brows rise toward my hairline. "Wow … I don't …" I'm not sure what to say.

"Don't get too shocked yet. There's still more." She clasps a locket hanging around her neck, dazing off momentarily. "The game's title is very fitting, since it's basically a bunch of deadly games that the participants have to play."

"Does anyone die?"

"Yep."

My chest tightens. "Oh."

"Not everyone, though. Ollie, Phoenix, and Roman participate every year since even before they came to this academy. And while they've never won, they also come out fine. Or, well, as fine as they ever are."

"But if the participants are picked at random, then how do they end up getting selected every year?"

"Yeah, I think they rig it. But, being who they are, no one questions it."

My confusion meets a new-time high. "Why would they want to be part of that?" Unless they're crazy. Maybe they are.

She gives a half-shrug. "Probably because they're after the crown. It's the prize the winner gets. It contains a drop of power from every creature that's ever existed, which means that the creature who possesses it has a drop of power from every creature. And that basically means they can pretty much do whatever they want."

Well, that sounds lovely.

"Don't the death triplets do that already?"

"To an extent. But this will make them even more powerful."

A shudder runs through me. At least, I imagine it does. For some weird reason, my body feels very numb at the moment.

"That sounds scary."

"It does," she agrees with a nod, slowing to a halt in front of a gigantic, arched doorway that stretches toward … the clouds above us?

Clouds?

Since when are there clouds in a school?

"Thankfully, they don't seem like they're going to win anytime soon." She clears her throat. "Now, enough talk about my brother and his stupid friends. It's time to introduce you to my favorite place at this school." She gives a dramatic gesture at the doorway. "Haven, I'd like to introduce you to the most wonderful library you'll ever set your eyes on."

I glance at the doorway, not seeing anything but clouds. But then, as if a magic veil has been lifted, the clouds start to evaporate, revealing towering bookshelves stretching as far as my eyes can see. And each shelf is packed with books, thick and thin, softback and hardback and even some leather-bound.

"Holy freakin' motherships," I mumble as I step inside and onto the misty floor. "It's like the internet of books."

"I'm not sure what the internet is, but this library is definitely awesome," she agrees as she steps in beside me.

"It's more than awesome," I say in awe as my gaze travels across everything, the shelves, the misty floor, the branches dangling from the ceiling. "What's with the tree branches?"

"The trees are what give us the knowledge that's put into the books." She gives me a *duh* look. She cocks her head to the side. "Where do humans get their book knowledge?"

I shrug, gaping in awe as one of the branches swoops down and places a book on a shelf. "From people."

"But then, how do you know it's true? People can lie, right?"

"Yeah, they do it all the time."

"So then, your books lie?"

"I ..." I pause as her words sink in. "You know what? I've never thought about it that way, but I guess you might be right."

She frowns at that. "Then, how do you know any of the truths?"

I shrug, my head feeling sort of fuzzy, probably from all the mist. "Maybe the human world is one big lie."

"Maybe," she agrees, a smile curling at her lips. "It definitely sounds boring."

"Compared to this …" I shake my head as another branch ravels down and grabs a book from the shelf, pulling it up into the sky. "Yeah, it's definitely boring … Where did it just take that book?"

"To someone who checked it out," she says matter-of-factly when nothing about this place is matter of fact.

"Come on," she says, motioning for me to follow her as she walks forward, farther into the room. "Let's go see if we can find some books about your kind."

Nodding, I trail after her, still gawking at everything. I'm sure my stunned reaction doesn't help me blend in, which is what I'm supposed to be trying to do, but I also don't see anyone else around, so I'm not too worried. Although, I am wondering …

"Where is everyone?" I ask as I move up beside her. "I mean, I know hardly any students are at the academy yet, but doesn't this library have librarians."

She tosses me a questioning look. "What're librarians?"

"Um … people who work at libraries and take care of all the books. Like checking them out to people and shelving them and stuff."

"Oh. Yeah, those are the trees. We just call them knowledge keepers, though."

So the trees are the librarians here. What a strange, strange world I'm in now.

She suddenly smiles. "The look on your face right now is so priceless."

"Sorry. I just can't get over all this." I gesture at the trees, the shelves, the clouds in the sky where lightning is zapping.

Holy crap, I wonder if it ever rains in here? If so, how do the books not get wet? And how do you even get the tree branches to collect books for you? And check them out? How does all this work?

I'm about to ask her all those questions when she suddenly turns toward me and places a finger to her lips. "For the next couple of minutes, we need to be super quiet."

I have no clue why, but I nod anyway.

She lowers her finger from her lips, sneaks a glimpse around, and then ducks into a gap between two bookshelves. I follow, the trees branches slipping out of my sight as we steal into the shadows of the shelves.

We walk quickly down a row of shelves, the air growing foggier and darker. By the time she finally comes to a stop, I can barely see past the fog. I'm about to ask her what's going on when I spot a thick, wooden door covered with padlocks on the other side of her. She flicks another glance around then snaps her fingers. A soft *poof,* and then her wand appears in her hand.

My eyes widen, but I seal my lips together, remembering that she told me to be quiet.

Lifting her wand, her lips move as she chants something silently. The end of her wand illuminates, and then the padlocks all unlock and the door opens. She steps inside, and I follow, letting a breath of relief slip out of me.

I'm not sure what I expected to be on the other side of the door, but all I see are more bookshelves. However, the cloudy sky is gone, replaced by darkness. I'm not sure if it's just a painted ceiling or emptiness.

As the door closes behind me, I figure I'm good to speak, but when I part my lips, she throws me a warning look. Then she gives a pressing glance around at the shelves. That's when I see them, glowing eyes peering out at us from behind the books.

My chest tightens as I hold my breath. What the hell are those things? I desperately want to ask but keep my lips zipped and follow Harper as she hurries down the aisle, her gaze skimming along the books.

Fog dances around us, spinning mugginess into the air. Above, the darkness shifts, hissing. Panic pulsates through me, but I try to be as calm as I can. It starts to get really difficult, though, when Harper comes to a stop in front of one of the bookshelves and lets out a quiet, shaky breath.

She's afraid, this faerie who didn't even so much as blink when the death triplets tried to intimidate her. And her fear becomes even more evident as she slowly reaches for a thick, leather-bound book labeled *The History of Maddenings: The Destruction of the Balance Realm.*

I have no idea what the Balance Realm is, but maddenings clearly destroyed it.

I don't get too much time to dwell on that, because Harper suddenly moves quickly, grabbing the book and reeling toward me.

"Run," she says with wide eyes.

It's the first word we've spoken in minutes, and I become aware of just how silent this area of the library is. But that silence dissolves as the creatures with those glowing eyes emerge from the shelves.

Four legs, grey fur, pointy ears, they're not very big, maybe the size of a large cat, but their claws are razor sharp. So are their teeth.

"Run!" Harper shouts this time then shoves me forward.

Snapping out of my trance, I reel around and run like hell. The movement must set the creatures off, because they suddenly launch themselves at us, fangs glinting, drool and growls leaking from their mouths.

Panic flares through my veins as I duck left then right, skittering to the side and jumping over one of them. As I near the door, I quicken my pace.

Just a little farther. Hopefully, anyway.

Wait. What if they chase us out the door—

Pain suddenly splinters through my arm as one of the creatures clips me with their claws. I whimper out in pain, but bitch-smack it away from me and keep running, stumbling out the door. Harper is right behind me, and the second she gets out of the room, she spins around, points the wand at the door, and shouts, *"Claude ostium!"*

I spin around just in time to see dozens of those creatures barreling at us. But right as they reach the doorway, the door slams shut and the deadbolts lock.

Harper lowers her wand and turns toward me, hugging the book to her chest, her eyes wide.

"Let me guess," I say, struggling to breathe evenly with my hand pressed against the wound on my arm. "That was the deadly and forbidden section of the library."

She bobs her head up and down. "I've never actually been in there before, which is probably a good thing. Otherwise, I would've really thought twice about going in there just now."

"Yeah." As the cut on my arm begins to throb, I lower my hand to look at the wound. Blood is trickling out of it, but it's already healing, which is so weird.

"Shit, did you get bit?" she asks, stepping toward me, worry flooding her features.

I shake my head. "One of those creatures' claws nicked me."

She visibly relaxes. "Oh, good. You should be okay in a few minutes, then." She squints at the wound. "In fact, I think it's already almost healed now, so I guess maddenings are immortal."

So I'm immortal.

Immortal.

I still can't wrap my head around it.

"Does that mean I can never die?" I ask.

She shakes her head. "Nah, it just means it's really hard to kill you."

"Oh." I glance at the wound again then back at her. "What would've happened if one of those creatures had bitten me?"

The frown that forms on her face makes me almost regret asking. "Then you would've turned into one of those monsters yourself. And you'd be stuck in there, guarding those books for the rest of your life. Considering you're probably immortal or close to it, that would be a very, very long time."

I swallow hard. "Are you saying that all those creatures in there are students who snuck into that room?"

"Yep," she says so casually, as if this is an everyday sort of thing.

But it's not. At least not for me.

Although, I do note that I'm not quite as shocked as I feel I should be. It makes me wonder if, at some point, perhaps one day, I'll get used to all this.

But, as I glance down at my wound again and see that it's completely healed, shock whips through me. So, maybe not.

HAVEN

AFTER HARPER AND I LEAVE THE BOOKSHELVES, SHE TAKES me to a sitting area in the library. In a human library, this area would probably consist of a couple of tables and chairs, but in The Monster Academy for the Magical's library, this consists of a massive fireplace, fancy rugs, and the most comfortable sofas I've ever sat on. And to add to the comfort, Harper somehow got hot chocolate and cookies delivered to us by what she told me was a sprite. To me, it just looked like a tiny faerie with glittering, silver wings.

"Sprites are cute," I say after the faerie flies away. I pick up a mug of hot chocolate and breathe in the sweet aroma. So yummy. It even has marshmallows in it.

"They may be cute, but their bites hurt like a bitch," she informs me as she collects the other mug of hot chocolate.

She's sitting across from me in a lounge chair that's right in front of the fireplace where a fire is crackling.

I feel comfortable, which is weird since, only about half an hour ago, I was bitten by some sort of rabid creature that apparently spends its entire existence guarding the deadly and forbidden section of the library.

I take a sip of my hot chocolate and, holy hell, it's the most delicious thing I've ever tasted.

"Do you turn into one of them if they bite you?"

She shakes her head, taking a drink of the hot chocolate before setting the mug down on a table between us. "Nah. It's not like those little devils in the forbidden and deadly section."

"Do those things have a name?"

"I don't know if there's an official name, but creatures in this school call them cursed fuckers." She cracks a smile.

I can't help laughing. "So, cursed fuckers' bites will turn you into one of them. Are there any other creatures' bites that can do that?"

She nods, opening the book we stole that has information about maddenings. "Werewolves, vampires, certain types of demons—the list goes on and on." She starts flipping through the pages.

I wonder what she's reading, what it says about my kind. I wonder if she'll be afraid of me after we get done going through that book.

"Okay." I give myself a beat to grasp that. "Phoenix is a vampire, right?"

She turns a page then glances up at me. "Yeah, he is. I don't think he's ever bitten anyone to turn them, though. He just does it to feed and for … pleasure." She looks down as she says that. If I didn't know any better, I'd swear a flush is spreading across her cheeks.

I remember Ollie saying that Phoenix has a thing Harper. From the look on her face, I have to wonder if she might like him, too.

"Have you guys ever dated?" Wait. Do monsters date?

She promptly shakes her head. "Gods, no." She lets out a laugh, but it sounds kind of forced and off-pitch.

Even stranger, the noise echoes inside my head.

So weird.

"I couldn't even imagine dating one of my brother's friends," she continues, reaching for her mug of hot chocolate.

I take another sip of mine and warmth spreads through my body as I swallow it. I sit back in the chair, feeling so relaxed that I swear I could fall asleep.

"He is really gorgeous, though," Harper confides then takes a drink from the mug. "Maybe if he wasn't my brother's friend …" She trails off with a dreamy look in her eyes.

"You'd what?" I ask, my voice sounding far away.

"I don't know." She shrugs, staring off into space.

It feels like I should keep talking, but my lips feel heavy. My body is also craving another sip of hot chocolate.

I lift the mug to my lips and down another gulp. "This stuff is yummy," I tell her.

She nods in agreement, her gaze floating to me. "You sound weird."

"So do you." I set the mug down. Well, I try to, but it falls from my fingers and lands on the floor, spilling all over the rug. "Crap." I move to stand up so I can clean it but, like my lips, my body feels heavy.

"It's fine. Someone will come clean it up," she says, her gaze dropping to the glittering puddle of hot chocolate on the floor.

Wait. Glittering? Since when does hot chocolate glitter? Maybe it has magic in it?

"Oh no," she abruptly mutters, rolling off the sofa and crawling over to the spilled mess on the floor, the book tucked underneath her arm.

"What's wrong?" I manage to roll off the sofa and kneel down beside her.

She squints at the puddle then pales as she looks at me. "Do you feel funny? Like lightheaded and stuff?"

I nod. "Yeah, kind of."

"Crap." She starts crawling across the floor. "Come on; we need to get out of here."

I follow her, crawling, too, but it's complicated, since my body just wants to lie down. "Why? What's going on?"

"I think a spell was laced into our drinks," she says in a lazy panic as she crawls toward the exit doors, using one arm because she refuses to put the book down.

"Like we were roofied?" I ask in horror, ducking low as a tree branch swoops down to collect a book on a lower shelf, but I don't move fast enough, and it ends up bumping me on the head. I barely feel it, and that makes alarms go off through the haziness in my mind.

"I don't know what that is," Harper tells me, her arms suddenly collapsing. She ends up just lying there on the floor, the book still cradled in her one arm.

Feeling super tired myself, I lie down beside her. "Did the sprite do this to us?"

"I don't know," she whispers. "Honestly, I'm kind of hoping it was her."

"You know what they say about hoping, Harper." A voice rises through the haze dancing around Harper and me.

She tilts her head to look up. So do I.

Looming over us is Phoenix, his fangs on full display.

"You did this to us?" Harper sluggishly shakes her head and glares at him. "I should've known."

Phoenix flashes her a toothy grin. "Now, baby, you should know by now that I never do anything this fun alone."

That's when Ollie and Roman step out from the shadows of the bookshelves.

A chill manages to spill down my spine as Roman's dark eyes lock on me, a set of black, feathery wings sprouting from his back. Each black feather has a blood-red tip, like it's been dipped in blood. I wonder if that's exactly what happened. If that's the blood of all the creatures he's hurt.

And that's the last thought I have before I black out.

HAVEN

"FREAK! NO ONE CARES ABOUT YOU!" THE KID SHOUTS, throwing a rock at me.

It hits me in my back, and pain splinters through my bones as tears sting my eyes.

I collapse to the ground and throw my arms protectively over my head as he throws another rock at me.

I was just minding my own business and hanging out by the slides by myself, like I always do at recess time, when a kid a couple of years older than me walked up and started throwing rocks at me while calling me a freak. He never said why, just kept doing it, almost like he was possessed.

Why does everyone always seem to hate me?

I'm not sure. All I know is that more kids crowd around me and start chanting, "Freak."

More rocks are thrown, and the pain in my back builds.

I wonder where a teacher is—where anyone is.

Why is this happening?

Why do they hate me so much?

Maybe I should make them pay.

The thought strikes me out of nowhere and, for the briefest moment, I see red. But then that pain in my back begins to build. It feels like my muscles are being pulled apart. I think I'm breaking apart from the inside out.

I'm breaking.

I'm broken—

Thump.

A rock pelts me in the head and everything goes black—

"What the hell is wrong with you guys?" Harper's voice slices through the memory that I'd almost forgotten.

I was six at the time and have never quite figured out what that pain in my back was. At the time, I thought it was from the rocks being thrown at me. But now, thinking back, I realize the pain had come from deep inside me and felt like it was trying to tear out of my shoulder blades.

"I'm not going to let you get away with this shit anymore," Harper continues to rage on as I slowly come to, my eyelids slowly lifting open.

It takes me a moment to realize I'm facedown on a rocky surface. I discreetly glance around and discover something that makes my gut twist.

I'm in a cave.

The Cave of Doom.

It doesn't look like an ordinary cave. Yeah, it has the same arched structure, but the rock it's made of looks like molten lava or something. Only, it's not hot. And I swear I can actually hear the cave growling from somewhere.

Maybe this is hell.

I need to get up and get out of here. But my arms and legs still feel numb. And I have no idea where everyone is. I mean, I can hear them and they sound close, but they must be standing on the other side of me.

"*Let us get away with it?*" Phoenix sneers. "Did you hear that, Rome? Harper thinks she has control over what we do."

"Then she's stupid," Roman says, sounding close. "No one controls us, and I think the fact that you're here, Harper, proves that."

Harper lets out a low laugh. "I can walk out of here whenever I want."

"True," Phoenix says. "But it'll just be you. She's not going anywhere."

By *she*, I'm sure he means me.

"Wanna bet?" Harper challenges. "You may think you're tough, vampire boy, but I can remember a little boy with fangs who used to cry over broken toys."

"Is that so?" A dangerous challenge etches into Phoenix's tone. "Because I can remember a time when a little dark faerie had a crush on me."

"*Had* being the keyword," Harper quips without missing a beat. "Now when I look at you, I just want to throw up."

"Come on, guys," Ollie gripes. "Can't we just all get along?"

"No!" Harper and Phoenix say simultaneously.

Ollie mutters something under his breath.

"That's enough," Roman interrupts in a firm tone. "I didn't go through all this work just to hear you guys bitch."

"No, you went through all this work because you're an asshole," Harper growls at him. "Now let her go before I walk out of here and report you."

Roman lets out a chilling laugh that glazes across my skin. "Go ahead. You know as well as I do that nothing will happen to us. Because no one will care what happens to her."

No one will care.

No one cares about you.

It feels like I'm on that playground all over again, only without the rocks being thrown at me. Although, my body does ache a bit.

"I care," Harper insists. "And if you hurt her, I'll make sure you pay."

"Is that so?" Roman says with a taunt in his tone.

"Oh, don't look at me like that with that cruel smile, Roman," she snaps. "Like Ollie, I remember all sorts of shit that would possibly ruin that bad boy title you worked so hard to obtain if I decided to tell everyone."

"Go ahead and try," Roman says. "I won't let you get very far."

"Rome," Ollie warns.

Roman talks over him. "Why the hell are you even defending her, Harper? You know what she is. You know what she's capable of. Are you really going to risk everything just to protect her? It's not worth your time. She's not worth your time." A drop of silence ticks by. "So make the smart choice here, go back to your dorm, pretend you never met her, and let us take care of her."

When Harper doesn't say anything right away, my heart breaks a little.

No one cares about you.

No one wants you.

Killer.

Pain.

So much pain.

Why am I in so much pain?

"I'm not going to do that," Harper whispers shakily. "She's not bad, Roman. And if you'd give her a chance—"

"*Give her a chance?*" he snaps. "Yeah, my brother said the same thing to me right before a maddening killed him!"

And there it is.

The reason he hates me so much.

I am a killer.

A monster.

And I'm breaking inside.

Splitting apart.

And maybe this is how it should be.

Maybe I should die.

As the blinding pain in my back builds, I think maybe that's what's going to happen. That I'm going to die right there on the cave floor.

I try to be quiet about it, try to conceal the agony tearing through me, but it finally bursts from my lips as a whimper escapes.

I push up, wishing I could crawl away from the pain, even though it's searing from inside me.

When I angle my head up, Roman is right in front of me with his wings spanned out. And just behind him, Phoenix is standing by Harper with his fangs on display, and Ollie is beside them, his shimmering eyes huge.

"What the hell is happening to her?" Ollie whispers.

Phoenix slowly shakes his head. "I don't know, but look at her back."

Harper's gaze darts to my back, and she gasps, covering her mouth.

I wonder what I look like, if perhaps the pain is eating me alive and I have a giant hole in my back.

That makes my stomach clench and vomit burns my throat.

"Something's wrong," Roman mutters, his dark eyes drinking me in.

A little less horror is present in his gaze than in the others, but he's definitely worried about something.

My thoughts immediately become distracted as something in my back cracks. *Bones?* I'm not sure, but I let out a pain-laced cry as my back contorts upward in a way it definitely shouldn't be able to bend.

"I think I'm dying," I whisper hoarsely, tears burning my eyes and sweat beading my skin. I'm not really talking to them, though. I'm telling myself that I think the end is near.

Death, Haven. You are it, and now it's going to consume you.

"No, you're not," Roman mutters, crouching down beside me. He tilts his head to the side and starts to reach for me, but then he jerks back and goes very pale as the sound of tearing fills the air. Then a loud *snap* echoes throughout the cave.

And suddenly, the pain is gone.

But something is different. My back feels heavier, as if a heavy object has been placed on me. And I think I might have a couple of holes in the back of my shirt, since I can feel air touching my skin back there.

"What the hell?" Ollie gapes at me then looks at Roman. "Why the hell does she have wings? She's a maddening. They don't have fucking wings."

My eyes snap wide, and my hand flies toward my back. The second my fingers brush against the soft feathers, panic seizes me. "Oh my God." I spring to my feet to run, like I can somehow outrun the damn things. Instead, I stumble from how off balance the extra weight makes me and trip forward right into Roman.

I expect him to move out of the way, but he must be in shock or something, because he remains frozen, and I end up landing right on top of him. He goes down hard, too, landing on his back, his wings spread out across the ground.

I scramble to get up, but the weight of the wings throws me forward and causes me to fall down and on top of him … again.

He curses as our bodies collide, moving his hands up to my waist and wrapping his fingers around me, probably preparing to throw me off him.

I quickly sit up and smack his hands off me. "Don't touch me." I feel helpless, because I can't get up, and it's pissing me off.

He holds his hands in front of him as he looks up at me. "I was just going to help you get off me." His gaze strays across my wings, and those shadows appear on his skin, twirling and spinning, like they're excited or something. Every time that's happened, it's right before he's about to do something awful to me.

I need to get out of here.

"*Help me?* Yeah right. I highly doubt that." Sucking in a breath, I move to get off him, but again, that extra weight throws me forward.

My fingers curl inward as frustration pulsates through me.

"Just let me help you," Roman says, inching his hands cautiously toward me.

He's being semi-nice, which more than likely means it's a trick. And I'm not about to fall for another one of those, so I dive off him and smack my cheek against the floor.

"Ow," I gripe as I roll to my side and press my hand to my cheek.

Dammit, this molten lava rock is harder than normal rock.

"Gods, would you just let me help you stand up?" Roman bites out as he pushes to his feet then reaches for me again.

Our eyes lock. He looks partly annoyed and partly scared out of his mind. Why? Oh, who the hell knows? I definitely don't care.

I glare at him. "Get away from me."

He narrows his eyes and parts his lips. "I—"

"Just leave her alone," Harper interrupts as she appears by my side, smacking his hand away.

Roman glowers at her. "I wasn't going to hurt her."

"Oh, I know you weren't," she assures him as she reaches down and grabs my arm. "But just because she has wings now that doesn't erase all the bullshit you did to her yesterday and today." Carefully, she helps me to my feet.

I wobble like a baby deer, but she holds on to me, her grip surprisingly strong.

"You're not going to have her. I don't give a shit if you were looking for this. You don't deserve her." She raises her chin defiantly.

Those shadows on his skin start to dance again as his eyes darken, and he curls his hands into fists.

Harper smirks at him. "Go ahead and do whatever you're about to do. I dare you."

I gape at her. What the heck is she doing, taunting him like that? I'm not sure what sort of powers he has, but Roman is clearly a dangerous creature.

We should just leave. Now. Get away from them and this cave. And get these wings off my back.

Wings.

Oh my God, I have wings!

I shake my head as reality sets in.

Harper gives me a pressing look that I don't even know how to decipher. Then she fixes her attention back on Roman, as if waiting for something to happen.

The muscles in his jaw tick, those shadows seeming to reach out of his body, but then he steps back. "Fine, you can leave," he tells her, seemingly with a lot of effort.

Throwing him another smirk, she turns us toward the domed exit of the cave. Then, holding on to me, she moves me forward with her.

"Just please keep an eye on her," Roman calls out. "You

know what this means. No one can find out about this, Harper. It's fucking dangerous if those wings mean what I think it mean."

I expect Harper to throw a snarky comeback at him, but all she does is say, "I know, and I will."

With that, she steers us out of the cave, leaving me to wonder what's so dangerous about me having wings. Better yet, why that made the death triplets back off from their plans of destroying me.

HAVEN

THE MOMENT WE EXIT THE CAVE, HARPER LEANS ME AGAINST the wall.

"Hold on. I need to put a spell on us before we head down the hallway." She snaps her fingers, and her wand appears in her hand.

"Why?" I ask as I prop my shoulder against the wall. I want to lean back against it, but it feels weird to have my wings against something. Kind of ticklish.

Wings are ticklish.

Wings.

I still can barely wrap my head around it.

I wonder if this is how things are going to be from now on—surprises and dangers constantly happening around me. I have a feeling it might, and I'm not sure how I feel about it. Although, I guess both stuff was present in my old life. It was just different kinds of dangers and surprises.

"I don't want to risk anyone seeing your wings," she informs me as she faces me with her wand pointed at me.

"Because I'm supposed to be a witch?" I ask, brushing some dirt off my arm.

She wavers, chewing on her bottom lip. "Let's just get back to the room, and I'll explain it to you."

"Okay," I agree.

Releasing a breath, she points the wand at me, muttering something under her breath. Sparks hiss from the tip, and then she lowers her wand.

"All right, no one should be able to see us now." She snaps her fingers again, and her wand dissolves into thin air. Then she reaches for me, grabs my arm, and steadies me before we start down the wide hallway lined with lanterns and black walls.

This ceiling is painted with a mural of mist and smoke that takes the form of hands. Eyes hide in the mistiness. It's kind of creepy.

"This place seems darker than the rest of the academy," I note as I grip her arm to keep from falling.

"That's because it leads to The Cave of Doom," she explains, quickening her pace, her gaze skimming the area as if something might suddenly jump out at us.

"Why is it called that?" I wonder as I struggle to keep up with her. "I mean, it didn't seem like anything doom-like happened back there. Well, except for me getting wings, but that ..." I look at her. "Wait—is that why I have wings now? Did the cave do this to me?"

She shakes her head, but then she hesitates. "Well, maybe." She blows out a breath, her muscles wound up in knots. "The Cave of Doom is supposed to extract the darkness out of a creature and haunt them with it. Or, well, if someone says the right incantation to trap you there. But no one said it, yet your wings appeared. I don't really think that's because of the cave, though. I think it might have been just a weird coincidence."

"So, you think my wings are real, then?" I frown when she nods. "Why do you think I suddenly have them?"

"I think somehow the cave's powers extracted your hidden death angel blood and tried to use it against you. How exactly, I'm not sure."

My brows knit, worry trickling through me. "Wait ... Death angel blood? I thought I was a maddening?"

"You are," she says. "But, apparently, you also have some hidden death angel blood inside you."

I swallow hard. "You mean, like Roman?"

She gives a hesitant nod. "Yeah, I think so." She pauses, wariness creeping into her features. "And I have to ask; did you know you had another bloodline in you?"

I shake my head. "No. I already told you and Jude that I didn't even realize I was a monster until I showed up here." I pause, recalling the memory I had when I was lying on the cave floor. "Although, there was this one time on the playground when I was being …" I pause, unsure if I want to talk about when I was tormented. "Well, some stuff was happening, and I felt like something was trying to break out of my back. I was actually having a dream about it right before I woke up in that cave."

"That's weird," she murmurs with a crease between her brows.

"Does it mean anything?"

"I'm not sure." She grows quiet, staring ahead as we hurry through the empty hallways.

"They're going to go away, right?" I sound strained as my back starts to ache from all the weight. "The wings, I mean."

Please say yes, because I can't imagine walking around with these things on my back. In fact, I want them to go away right now so I can forget about them. Forget just how big of a freak I am.

Her gaze flicks to me, and her expression softens. "Yeah, they will. We'll have to figure out how to do that, and maybe get some help, but I'm guessing they're like Roman's, and he keeps his tucked away most of the time."

"Okay." I let out a relieved breath.

"But," she adds cautiously, "I may have to get some outside help to figure out how, since I know absolutely nothing about death angels."

"You know more than just Roman, right?" I ask hopefully.

She offers me an apologetic look. "Not really. I mean, I know his family, but they're all a bit …" She trails off, shrugging and leaving me to wonder what Roman's family is like.

Are they bad, like Roman? Is that why he is the way he is?

I remember something then, something I overheard.

"A maddening killed Roman's brother?" I ask, but it's not really a question.

Her eyes slightly widen. "You heard that?"

Pressing my lips together, I nod. "That's why he hates me, right?"

"He doesn't hate you." She gives my arm a gentle squeeze. "He doesn't know you well enough to feel hate toward you. His family is just very prejudice toward your kind."

"I guess that's understandable."

"No, it's not. Just because one creature killed someone doesn't mean all creatures of that kind will, too. If that's how things worked, then we'd all be killers."

A killer.

I haven't killed anyone yet, but I've hurt people. And, isn't that like a step toward becoming a killer? I'm not sure, but I'm worried. Maybe if I knew more about who I am and where I came from, I could figure it out.

"Off the subject, but do you still have that book we stole?" I ask, hoping she does so maybe I can figure out more about myself and my kind.

A grin pulls at her lips. "Of course I do. We worked too hard for me to lose it."

"Where is it, then?"

"Before the guys dragged us to that cave, I used a spell and sent it to the room."

I smile at that. "You're kind of awesome."

She grins. "Oh, I know I am. But so are you."

"Why? I didn't even do anything."

"You stood up to Roman and, considering the situation"—she wavers—"it was pretty damn awesome."

My brows pull together. "What situation?"

She rubs her lips together, contemplating. "Let's save that one for another time. Right now, we need to focus on getting those wings tucked away before anyone else sees them."

She stops in front of a door, and I realize we've made it to our dorm room already.

"But, shouldn't we be worried that the death triplets will tell everyone what I am?" I ask as she opens the door.

Shaking her head, she helps me inside and across the room, only letting me go when I grab a table to keep my balance. Then she heads back to the door and shuts it. "Trust me; they won't tell anyone," she assures me as she locks the door.

I steady myself then stand up straighter. "How can you be so sure?"

She shucks off her jacket and tosses it onto the sofa. "That's part of the save that for another time."

She's being so vague and, while I want to press her for more details, I'm more focused on getting these wings put away first since they're extremely heavy.

"Let me go grab my handheld so I can do a search and see if there's any information I can find on how death angels put their wings away." She starts across the room, heading toward her bedroom doorway. "I really doubt it, but it's a starting point."

When she steps into the room, I decide I should probably try to sit down before my legs give out on me.

As I stumble my way toward the sofa, I catch a glimpse of my reflection in a mirror on the wall. Through all the madness that happened, I didn't even try to look at my wings. Now, I can't look away.

The girl in the mirror, I barely recognize her—big eyes; long, dark hair. My face looks the same, yet it doesn't, as if magic was sprinkled all over me. And then there are the wings. The massive, feathery wings spanning out from my back. They almost look exactly like Roman's—black with red tips. The only difference is that, at the right angle, mine have a slight iridescent glow to them. They're freaky to look at coming out of me.

When I twist around to get a better look, I see that I do

have two giant holes in my shirt from where the wings snapped out. I wouldn't really care—I mean, it's just a shirt—but I only have a few shirts total, and now I have one less.

"They're really pretty." Harper appears behind me, holding her handheld device.

"I was kind of just thinking that," I admit, reaching around and lightly touching the velvety feathers. "They're kind of freaky, too, though."

She shakes her head. "Nah. It's just something that'll take some time getting used to."

"I hope so." I lower my hand. "Why do they look so much like Roman's? Or do all death angels have the same wings?"

"No, they're all different."

A thought occurs to me then. "Is it because we might be related?"

"No, that's not how it works, either." She considers something then shakes her head and steps up beside me. "I don't want to freak you out, but there's one thing I need to say." Worry suddenly floods her expression. "Because you have maddening powers and these wings, it means you're a hybrid. And that can be a very dangerous thing. Not because you're dangerous, but because you're part of the unknown. And creatures generally tend to fear the unknown."

I think back to my time in the human world and how

much everyone feared me because I was different. "I know."

She offers me a sad smile. "So, I think, for now, this needs to stay just between you and me and the death triplets. I don't even think we should tell Jude."

"Okay." I pause. "Are you sure we can trust the death triplets?"

She doesn't even miss a beat when she nods.

I have no clue how she can be so confident about this after everything that's happened, but I decide to trust her. I just hope I'm not making a huge mistake.

HAVEN

A LONG TIME LATER—I STILL HAVEN'T FIGURED OUT THE whole compass time thing—my wings are still out and both Harper and I are starting to get really frustrated. We've tried almost everything to get them to go back into my back, from spells to salves, but the damn things want to stay out and be all pretty and on display.

We're sitting on the sofa, and she's massaging her temples with her fingertips, her head lowered. "Good gods, this is giving me a headache."

I didn't realize faeries could get headaches. Apparently, though, they can. So can maddenings and death angels since I'm getting one, too.

"Me, too," I agree, reaching up and massaging my shoulder. "My back's really starting to hurt, too."

She lowers her hands from her temples and looks at me.

"Headaches and backaches aside, I'm also starting to worry someone's going to show up here and see your wings. Jude's supposed to be coming over later." She tucks a strand of hair behind her ear and frowns. "I hate to say this, but I think we might need some help."

I immediately frown. "From Roman, you mean?" He's the last creature I want to see.

She sighs heavily. "Yeah, I think so."

I crinkle my nose but don't protest.

When she sees the look on my face, she adds, "We can just call him on this." She taps the handheld device sitting on her lap. "He doesn't need to come over. Although, he's probably going to try."

I don't even ask why this time. Every time she brings up Roman and I ask a question about it, she tells me that's part of the "save it for another time."

Blowing out a loud breath, she sits up straighter then cracks her knuckles. "All right, let's do this." She taps a few buttons on the screen, and then it starts buzzing.

A couple of buzzes later, there's a *click* and then a, "Took you longer than I expected."

Roman sounds amused, which is a different tone for him, I realize. From my experience, he usually only sounds annoyed.

"Yeah, well, I was trying to figure it out on my own," Harper replies in an irritated tone. She frowns, glancing at me then back at the screen. "So, how do we do it?"

"Do what?" he asks, but I can tell he knows what she means.

"Don't play dumb with me, Roman," she snaps. "You know what I mean."

"All right, maybe I do," he admits. "But I think you know that I'm not going to just help. I want something out of it."

"Yeah, I figured as much," she mutters with a frown. "What do you want from me?"

"What?" I hiss, not wanting her to give him anything.

She holds up a finger, indicating for me to be quiet.

"I don't want anything from you," Roman replies. "Again, I think you probably already know that."

Her jaw clenches as she shakes her head. "Just spit it out, Roman. Stop toying with us."

He pauses, not answering her right away. "I want her to be on our team during the games."

"What?" I stammer at the same time Harper says, "No fucking way."

"Would you two relax? It's not that big of a deal," he says with a hint of annoyance.

"Not that big of a deal?" Harper gapes at the screen. "She barely knows about our world and her powers. She wouldn't stand a chance on surviving." She pulls a whoopsie face and glances at me, mouthing, *"Sorry."*

"It's fine," I whisper. "You're just saying the truth."

"I know, but it's harsh."

"Well, the truth is harsh sometimes."

We grow quiet then. Even Roman remains quiet.

I just start to wonder if he hung up when he says, "Harper, you know I'm not going to let her get hurt. I just … I need the power to win the game."

"You say that like I would want you to win," Harper retorts. "I don't."

Another pause.

"What if I promised you that I wouldn't use the crown for anything harmful?" he says cautiously.

She rolls her eyes. "Then I'd say you're full of shit."

He hesitates. "I'd make a blood promise on it."

He must be telling the truth because Harper seems to be considering what he asks.

"And you'd promise she wouldn't get hurt?" she finally asks.

"You know I will," he answers without any hesitation.

Again, I'm left wondering what in the world is going on. Why is he suddenly so okay with protecting me instead of trying to hurt me?

Harper considers this for a little bit longer. "Fine," she finally caves. "But there's a couple of conditions. One, you make all the promises we just discussed. Two, you don't just teach her how to put her wings away; you teach her everything that has to do with death angels. And three, you guys bring her into your group."

My eyes bulge. "What? No. I don't want that."

"I know you don't want it," she tells me, "but you need it; trust me." She looks back at the screen on the handheld. "She doesn't have to hang out with you guys or anything. You just have to acknowledge that she's part of your stupid little group so no one will mess with her."

Okay, maybe that's not such a terrible idea.

"That's a lot to ask," Roman says with a bite of annoyance in his tone.

"Yeah, well, you're asking a lot, too," she throws back at him. "But I think, if you really think about this deal, you'll be okay with it." She looks at me. "I want you to be okay with it, too."

I'm not sure what to say. Honestly, I'm not sure I fully understand everything they're bargaining. But I do trust Harper.

"Do you think I should do it?" I ask her, shifting my weight.

She nods with zero reluctance. "I really do. I think this will give you some protection. Plus, he can help you figure out all your powers and stuff."

I'm still not totally on board with it, but I also know nothing about this world, my powers, or the academy, and she does.

I blow out an unsteady breath. "Okay. If you think I should do it, then I'll do it."

"Good." She returns her attention back to the screen. "Do we have ourselves a deal?"

He considers it, but not for very long. "Yeah, we have ourselves a deal. I'll be over in a minute."

"No, we can handle all the details tomorrow," she quickly says. "Jude's coming over soon and, right now, I just need to get her wings put away."

"So, what? You just want me to help her right now, and then just take your word on it that we'll seal this deal with a blood promise tomorrow?" he questions with cynicism. "Because, first of all, taking someone's word on a deal isn't my fucking style. And second, teaching her how to put her wings away will take some time. Now, there is a spell I can do that'll put them away, but she'll eventually have to learn to do it herself. And that still doesn't help my issue with just taking your word on all this."

She dramatically rolls her eyes. "I'm not sure why you won't just take my word. You know I know better than to screw you over."

"Well, up until yesterday, I would've thought you did," Roman says coldly. "But then you pulled that stunt with the maddening and took her from us."

"That maddening has a name," she snaps. "It's Haven. And you should probably start calling her that."

Silence skips between them.

"You're right," he finally says, speaking much more softly, something that's as weird as ... well, the wings on my back. "Fine, I'll take your word on this, but if you screw me over again, there will be consequences."

"Whatever. I won't, so I'm not worried," she says with an eye roll. "Now hurry up and get over here so we can get this done before Jude shows up." She moves to touch the screen with her fingertip. "And make sure it's just you. Ollie and Phoenix don't need to be here for this." With that, she shuts off the hand-held and slumps back on the sofa, letting out a loud exhale. "Well, that was fun." Sarcasm oozes from her tone.

"Sorry you had to do that," I tell her, wishing I could lean back and relax, but I can't for a few different reasons; one being that my wings are in the way, and another being that Roman is coming over.

A crease forms between her brows. "Why? It's not your fault."

"Um, yeah, it is," I disagree. "All of this is only happening because I'm here." Because I exist.

She dismisses me with a flick of her wrist. "I promise you that, if you weren't here, I'd still be having some sort of drama with my brother and his friends. It's sort of our thing."

"Really?" I ask, and she nods. "Why—"

My question is cut off by a knock on the door.

"Wow, that was fast," I mutter.

"Yeah, it was," she agrees, sitting up stiffly. "Maybe it's not him."

We trade an apprehensive look before she gracefully

gets to her feet. "Stay right there," she tells me then hurries over to the door.

"Who is it?" she calls out.

"Who do you think it is?" Roman's voice floats from the other side.

She visibly unstiffens then rolls her eyes as she unlocks the door and opens it. "That was fast." Her tone is all sorts of confusingly taunting.

Roman rolls his dark eyes. "Stop insinuating stuff."

"I'm not insinuating anything." She still sounds mocking, but she steps inside and motions for him to come in.

He pauses, which I find a little strange, but then he collects himself and strides right on in. The moment he enters, his gaze finds me and a ton of emotions flash across his face. So many that I can't even sort through them. His eyes skim along my wings before settling on my gaze. Then his expression turns guarded, those emotions dissolving.

"You didn't know you had death angel blood in you?" he questions warily.

Pressing my lips together, I shake my head. "I didn't even know I was a … maddening until I showed up here."

"Yeah, that's what we were told." Skepticism rings in his tone.

"Stop interrogating her," Harper intervenes, nudging him forward. "We're on a ticking compass, so chop-chop. Let's get her wings put away so you can leave."

Roman flits her a dark look but, strangely, doesn't

argue. Instead, he walks forward and sits down on the table in front of me so we're facing each other, our knees just inches apart.

Uncomfortable with how close he is, I start to scoot away.

"If this is going to work, I'm going to have to touch you," he tells me, rolling up the sleeves of his shirt.

I freeze, frowning. "Why?"

"Because that's how the spell works," he says with a shrug.

I look to Harper for confirmation, but she just shrugs, too.

"I have no idea if he's telling the truth or not," she says. "So, we're just going to have to take his word on it."

His lips quirk. "How ironic."

"Good gods, you're annoying," she mutters under her breath as she flops down in a nearby chair.

Roman just smirks then fixes his gaze on me. Shadows begin to dance across his skin, spinning and twirling.

"What are those shadows on your skin?" I ask, figuring maybe he'll explain since he's helping me.

"It's part of the death angels' power," he explains vaguely.

I nervously chew on my lip as I stare at the shadows on his tattooed arms. "Will it happen to me?"

His brows furrow. "I'm not sure. I mean, all death angels have it, but you're not completely a death angel."

I hesitate, debating whether or not to ask what I want, but then I decide I'm never going to figure out anything about myself if I don't.

"Do you …? I mean, have you ever heard of another creature like me?"

"I've heard of hybrids," he clarifies. "But I've never heard of a hybrid maddening and death angel." His features harden. "Usually, my kind aren't stupid enough risk procreation with your kind. Not always, though."

I wonder if he's talking about his brother.

Harper abruptly reaches forward and smacks Roman on the back of the head. "Stop talking to her like that," she warns, disregarding the death look Roman gives her. "I know you've had a bad experience with maddenings, but she barely knows anything about them. And she's part death angel, so calling it *your* and *her* kind isn't correct. It's hers, too."

He continues to glare at her. "Careful, Harper."

"No, thanks," she replies with a snarky grin.

He grits his teeth then looks back at me again. He assesses me momentarily with his head angled to the side, wisps of his dark hair hanging in his eyes. "She's right," he finally says. "You are part of my kind." Then, with a deep breath, he reaches toward me.

I instinctively jerk back.

He freezes with his hands extended forward. "If you

want to get those wings off your back, I'm going to have to do this," he says, losing patience.

I don't want him to touch me. At all. Sure, he's gorgeous. Like extremely gorgeous. And I know he's trying to help me, but the events of being locked in that cage, of being drugged and dragged to that cave, of the brutal words he said to me … they still haunt me.

Regardless, I know I need to get over it. At least enough to get these wings tucked away. So, sucking in an inhale, I slant forward until his hands touch my shoulders.

I can feel myself shaking from the inside and hope he can't. If he does, he doesn't let on, his expression never changing.

"Okay, I'm going to say the spell, and then you're gonna feel a little bit of my magic," he informs me, steadily carrying my gaze. "After that, your wings should be gone."

I give an uneven nod. "Will it hurt?"

He dithers. "My magic won't, but it might hurt a little bit when your wings go back in. It'll be less painful than when they came out."

I have so many questions, but knowing we don't have time for that right now, I just nod.

He starts to chant words in a different language, and those shadows begin to dance, twirling across his arms and up mine. I watch them in shock, unsure if that's what's supposed to happen. Then I feel it—his magic weaving through me—and, oh my God, it feels wonderful. There's no other way to describe it. Tingling and soft and somehow familiar, almost like it's a part of me.

It takes a lot of effort not to gasp, especially when my wings fold inward, my skin burning as the feathers slip back inside my shoulder blades. I squeeze my eyes shut and try to breathe evenly as pain nips through my body.

Just as quickly as the pain started, it stops.

I crack my eyes open and glance over my shoulder. The wings are gone.

"Oh, thank God," I breathe out, slumping back in the sofa.

Roman watches me, his dark eyes intense. "You may not like them now," he says quietly, "but you'll eventually trust them more than anything else in the worlds."

I rub at my shoulder. "You say that like they're an actual living thing."

He shakes his head. "No, but they're a huge part of you."

I want to ask him if it'll be easier to shift them in and out of me. I want to ask him if I can fly. I want to ask him so many things, but Harper jumps up from the sofa, snags his sleeve, pulls him to his feet, and then shoves him toward the door.

"Thanks for the help," she tells him. "But Jude is gonna be here in like ten minutes, so you need to leave."

"Fine," he says as she yanks the door open and tries to push him out of the room. "But I'll be back tomorrow to collect your debt and make that blood promise," he warns, and then his gaze strays to me. He presses his lips together, his expression softening ever so slightly.

She gives him a thumbs-up then slams the door in his face. Then she turns to me, crossing her arms, a confused smile playing on her lips.

"What's that look for?" I wonder as I stretch my arms above my head, feeling so much lighter.

She just shakes her head. "It's nothing." She moves toward the sofa. "I just have a feeling that this year, school is going to be a little bit different. Less intense."

Her statement seems to come out of nowhere.

I lower my hands. "Why do you think that?"

She picks up the handheld, that smile still present. "I just have a feeling the death triplets are going to be too distracted to torment creatures as much as they usually do, you know, now that they're technically the death four."

Her words knock the breath out of me.

"Wait … I never agreed that."

"Doesn't matter. You'll become part of them."

"How do you know?"

She looks back at the door then at me. "I just have a feeling."

She doesn't explain more, and then Jude shows up, so the conversation gets shut down. That doesn't mean I don't stop thinking about it. Just like I don't stop thinking about how good Roman's magic made me feel.

The latter is annoying and, for some reason, I get the

feeling there's more of a reason as to why I felt that way than I know. But, for now, I probably have bigger things to worry about.

Like the fact that, in a few days, I'm going to be officially starting classes at Monster Academy for the Magical.

ROMAN

I DON'T RETURN TO MY ROOM RIGHT AWAY, NOT WANTING TO go there until I've calmed down. If Ollie and Phoenix see me like this—all riled up and out of control—they're going to tease the hell out of me, more than they already have. In fact, the moment Harper took Haven out of the cave and the reality of the situation set in, they instantly started teasing me.

"How coincidental is that?" Phoenix had said with a grin. "Your wing match is half maddening."

Ollie was more sympathetic. "I'm sorry it turned out this way."

I wasn't sure if I was.

Honestly, I was just really confused. Still am.

We'd been looking for my wing match for a while, and I'd hoped they'd ended up being at the academy. Not because I wanted to find my other half or anything like that. What I want is their power so I can win the games, get that crown, and bring my brother back from the dead.

The problem is that Haven has no idea how to use her powers. Plus, she's part maddening.

Maddening.

I'm matched to a maddening.

As reality sets in, I duck into a nearby alcove and lean against the wall. My head is spinning as I try to process that information, process what that means.

"It doesn't have to mean anything," I mutter to myself. "Just because she's your match doesn't mean you have to be soulmates. You can just use her for her power."

It seems so easy but, as I take out the feather from my pocket, a feather that fell off her wing before she tucked them away, I'm not so sure it'll be as simple as I want.

The moment I saw her wings, I felt a connection to her. But it was purely because of the magic bound between us. It doesn't mean anything. Not anything real, anyway.

Besides, all magic, even wing match magic, can be broken, which is exactly what I plan on doing. Because I can't be matched to a maddening forever. Not just because of what happened to my brother, but if my parents found out, they would destroy Haven.

Sage smiled to herself as she leaned back in a chair and watched the screen on the wall. She was in her private room, watching footage from the cave that had been recorded earlier today.

While the school didn't have cameras everywhere, the more dangerous parts of the building were under surveillance. It didn't use to be that way, but then a girl died in The Cave of Doom and Mor decided some things needed to change.

And, while Sage sometimes found the cameras a great inconvenience due to the fact that they made it more complicated to sneak around, right now, she was positively ecstatic.

"I was right," she mused as she replayed the footage of the maddening's wings appearing.

She hadn't been sure if Haven was the maddening she was looking for. The legend of the hybrid had been told so many times that it was hard to tell what parts held truth and what parts were simply a story. But there she was, a maddening with feathered wings.

Although, the fact that her wings matched Roman's was going to pose a bit of a problem. She hadn't planned for that. She would figure out a way around it, even if she had to figure out a way to get rid of Roman. She wasn't about to let a spoiled death angel ruin her plans of getting a hybrid maddening. She would get her hybrid, and she would use her to win the deadly games and get that crown, even if it meant killing anyone who got in her way.

She smiled to herself as she thought that. She could almost taste the blood on her cold, dead tongue.

ABOUT THE AUTHOR

Jessica Sorensen is a *New York Times* and *USA Today* best-selling author who lives in the snowy mountains of Wyoming. When she's not writing, she spends her time reading and hanging out with her family.

For information: jessicasorensen.com

Monster Academy for the Magical:

Monster Academy for the Magical

Monster Academy for the Magical: Hidden Magic

Monster Academy for the Magical: The Monster Clique (coming soon)

Tangled Realms:

Untitled (coming soon)

Harlynn's Mystery Investigations:

Sugar Cookies & Zombie Secrets

Untitled (coming soon)

Curse of the Vampire Queen:

The Secret Life of a Vampire

Untitled (coming soon)

Mystic Willow Bay Mysteries Series:

The Secret Life of a Witch

Broken Magic

Stolen Kisses One Wild, Crazy, Zombie Night

Magical Whispers & the Undead

Untitled (coming soon)

<u>**Enchanted Chaos Series:**</u>

Enchanted Chaos

Charmed Chaos

Entangled Chaos

Untitled (coming soon)

<u>**Capturing Magic:**</u>

The Thief of Wishes

The Thief of Magic

Untitled (coming soon)

<u>**My Cursed Superhero Life:**</u>

Cursed

Untitled (coming soon)

<u>**Guardian Academy Series:**</u>

Entranced

Entangled

Enchanted

Entice

Charmed

Untitled (coming soon)

The Shattered Promises Series:

Shattered Promises

Fractured Souls

Unbroken

Broken Visions

Scattered Ashes

The Fallen Star Series:

The Fallen Star

The Underworld

The Vision

The Promise

The Lost Soul

The Evanescence

The Mist of Stars (untitled)

The Darkness Falls Series:

Darkness Falls

Darkness Breaks

Darkness Fades

The Death Collectors Series (NA and YA):

Ember X and Ember

Cinder X and Cinder

Spark X and Spark

Standalones:

The Forgotten Girl

The Honeyton Mysteries:

Chasing Hadley

The Deal & a Secret

Untitled (coming soon)

Rebels & Misfits Detectives Mysteries:

Spies, Lies, & Cupcakes

Secrets, Lies, & Sugar Kisses (coming soon)

My Life with the Band

Discovering Benton

Whispered Secrets & a Kiss

Untitled (coming soon)

The Sunnyvale Mysteries:

The Year of Truths & Kisses

The Year of Secrets & Love Confessions

The Year of Mystery & First Dates

The Year of Love & Whispered Truth

The Year of Promises & First Kiss

Untitled (coming soon)

The Mysteries of Star Grove

Suspicion

Untitled (coming soon)

Rules of Willow & Beck:

Untitled (coming soon)

The Confession of Luna:

The Confessions of Luna

Untitled (coming soon)

Lexi Ashford Series:

The Diary of Lexi Ashford

The Diary of Lexi Ashford: The Agreement

Untitled (coming soon)

The Heartbreaker Society:

Ash & the Guy Next Door

Ash & the Secret

Ash & the Mysterious Stranger (coming soon)

The Diaries of Callie: Volume 2 (coming soon)

The Diaries of Violet: Volume 3 (coming soon)

The Secret Series:

The Prelude of Ella and Micha

The Secret of Ella and Micha

The Forever of Ella and Micha

The Temptation of Lila and Ethan

The Ever After of Ella and Micha

Lila and Ethan: Forever and Always

Ella and Micha: Infinitely and Always

The Secret Star Grove Mysteries:

Ella & the Interrupted Road Trip

Ella & the Welcome Home

Breaking Nova Series:

Breaking Nova

Saving Quinton

Delilah: The Making of Red

Nova and Quinton: No Regrets

Tristan: Finding Hope

Wreck Me

Ruin me

<u>**Unbeautiful Series:**</u>

Unbeautiful

Untamed